DAVID ASHBY

GRIBBLEBOB'S BOOK OF UNPLEASANT GOBLINS

PUSHKIN CHILDREN'S

Pushkin Press

71–75 Shelton Street

London WC2H 9JQ

Copyright © 2019 David Ashby

First published by Pushkin Press in 2019

1 3 5 7 9 8 6 4 2

ISBN 13: 978-1-78269-234-8

Designed and typeset by Tetragon, London

Printed and bound by CPI Group (UK) Ltd, Croydon, CRO 4YY

www.pushkinpress.com

This book is for Elvira, Sam and Tilly,
without whom there wouldn't be a book
and I wouldn't be me.

CHAPTER 1

It probably started that Wednesday afternoon, the one when it rained and the sun shone at the same time and there was that long, echoey tumble of thunder. I guess, looking back, you could say it was a sign—or a portent, as Granny C liked to say. When there was sun and rain at the same time, Granny C said it meant that, somewhere, a dog and a cat were getting married. But then again, Granny C smelt of stale lavender sticks and dust, and always wore strange clothes from the charity shop. Mainly tartan.

Still, anyway, that's probably when it started.

The rain had stopped, but the sun was bright and sharp as a wasp's wing, and Anna and Nils were walking home from the park. Nils had fallen off the "whizz-wheel"—that's what he called it—and had scraped his knee a little, so he wanted to go home and get a Spider-Man plaster. They were walking along the dirt path that wound its way through Timberton Woods. Well, they called them "woods" but really it was just a small explosion of trees between the park and home. It was a bit odd they were there really, as there weren't any other trees close by, just this thick cluster of dark oaks, sweet chestnuts and silver birches. The children were on the bit of the path leading into the woods, when they noticed a little man walking ahead of them.

He was no taller than Anna—who wasn't very tall for her age anyway—and was walking in a very determined and speedy manner. He splashed through a puddle on the path and wobbled slightly, looking rather like a discombobulated penguin trying not to drop his best fish.

Nils raised his hand to point at the fast-moving figure, but Anna pushed it down and shushed him. One of their mum's best friends had a sister about the same size, who told really funny stories and had dyed-blue streaks in her spiky hair. They had met her once when Nils was quite young, and she'd explained that she was a "little person". Something had happened to her when she was in her mummy's tummy, so she didn't develop like other people. She explained there was nothing to be scared of and how she was used to people staring at her, but Mum told them afterwards that it isn't nice to stare or point or make fun of people just because they are a bit different.

The little man really was hurrying along the path, but he kept stopping and muttering every now and again, so the children had nearly caught up to him just before the path entered the woods. Then they noticed the really strange thing. He had a dog lead in his hand, which trailed down to where you might expect to see a dog, but there was nothing there. The collar the lead was attached to was just sort of... hanging there. Now, that wasn't the strange thing, as they had both seen novelty items like that before—you can get them in the party shop in town, the one next to the estate agents, and the lead is actually stiff plastic to make it look like you are taking an invisible dog for a walk. So, no, that wasn't the strange thing. The strange thing was that, in the bright sunshine, you could clearly see the little man's shadow and the shadow of the lead, but also the shadow of some sort of small dog trotting along besides him. The shadow of a dog that wasn't there!

At first, Anna thought the joke-shop leads were getting really clever, but then the dog (that wasn't there) did some type of sneezy bark. The little man yanked on the lead, bent down to the dog and grumbled loudly.

"Be quiet, Dimple! Bad dog. Bad, bad dog. I know you're hungry, but we're so late!"

As he had bent down he had also half turned, so he saw Nils and Anna just behind him.

"Oh crumblesnips," they heard him say, and then he quickened his pace and pulled hard on the lead. They saw the shadow legs of the dog that wasn't there—Dimple, I guess—move briskly with a quiet little bark of annoyance. The little man and his accompanying shadows moved faster along the path. The path turned as it entered the woods and the children lost sight of him.

"Come on," Anna said to Nils, "let's catch him up!" and they broke into a slight run.

Well, when they turned into the woods, the path straightened out and continued between the darkness of the trees, but they couldn't see the little man anywhere.

"Where's he gone?" asked Nils.

"Shh," said Anna, putting a finger to her lips and stopping Nils with her other hand. "Let's see if we can hear him," she whispered, and they were both quiet and still. They heard nothing, apart from scattered birdsong and a slight rustle of leaves in the breeze.

Nils bent down and picked up something from the path. "Do you think he dropped it?" he asked, handing the item over.

It was a tiny book, which just fitted into Anna's palm. The book was cracked, brown leather, and in fancy gold-leaf writing the title read:

Gribblebob's Book of Unpleasant Goblins and Other Unnecessary Shadowfolk

CHAPTER 2

Bengt Arbuthnot hated his name. He hated it much more than he hated school, and he hated school very much indeed. Well, that wasn't really fair, it wasn't school he hated—he hated Mandy Musgrave.

Mandy was a short, flat sort of a girl, with ribbony hair and flubbery lips that had a constant film of spit over them. Mandy was very funny and always had something to say that made everyone else, even the teachers, laugh. Unfortunately, she mostly had things to say about Bengt, although these were not in front of the teachers. Mandy thought that Bengt's name was especially funny. She often called him "Burnt-My-Butt-Off" or "Ben-No-Butt" or something else involving bottoms.

Bengt couldn't help his name. His mother was Swedish and his father's family had originally come from Yorkshire. His mother's grandfather had been called Bengt, his mother's father had been called Bengt, his mother was called Bengta, and she had been adamant when he was born that he was going to carry on the family tradition. His father wanted to call him Ian, which he thought was a good Yorkshire sort of name, and Bengt would have liked that: Ian Arbuthnot. Although Mandy might still have called him "Knee-in Your-Hard-Butt-Knot" or something like that. Still, it was what it was, and he was called Bengt Arbuthnot, and he hated his name and the parts of school involving Mandy Musgrave—and custard.

This particular day, he was sitting under his favourite tree—*Doesn't everyone have a favourite tree?* he wondered sometimes—with his little notebook, writing down possible alternative names that he might use when he got old enough to change his name by deed poll. *Jack Broadsword* was his current favourite, but he was also rather taken with *Oscar Oakheart* and *Will Sky*. Or maybe *Will Summersky?* So much to think about. His pen was poised to write down another name, something with "knight" in, when suddenly Bengt's world turned upside down.

There was a low, long dice-throw of thunder, and Bengt looked up at the warm, grey sky, just in time to see the bright flash of lightning arrowing straight at him. There was a sense of being pulled up, out of himself, of rollercoaster-tumbling, of slipping. He could still feel his notebook and pen in his hands, but then tiredness washed through him and his fingers relaxed, and the book and pen slipped away from him.

And everything changed.

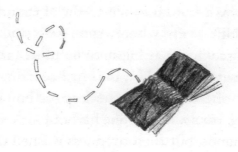

CHAPTER 3

"What's it about?" asked Nils. "'Unpleasant goblins.' What does that mean? Aren't all goblins unpleasant?"

"I don't know," Anna replied, turning the book over in her palm. "Perhaps not. Maybe some are more unpleasant than others," she said, smiling.

"Open it up, maybe there are pictures or something."

Anna tried to do as her little brother asked, but the book wouldn't open when she tried to pull the covers apart. It actually seemed to vibrate a little bit, like a wasp caught in an empty jam jar, angry and scared and slightly disappointed.

"It's locked," Anna said in surprise.

"Locked? Like your diary? But there's no pad-lock." Nils knew where Anna kept the key to her diary: under the big brown seashell she kept on her windowsill. Not that he had ever opened it when she was out, to check if she had written anything about him... (She hadn't.)

"I know, that's the strange thing. You try, maybe it's just me."

She handed the book over. As he took it, Nils looked up at her in wide-eyed surprise.

"It's fluttering or something!" he exclaimed. He too tried to open the book, but it remained stubbornly shut.

"Do you think it's got some type of battery-operated lock in it?" he asked. "Maybe that's why it's humming. Maybe you just need to press some-where," he guessed, and he started to jab at the book in random places, but all in vain.

"It looks a bit old to have a battery in it," said Anna, taking the book back from her brother. "But it is really strange that we can't open it."

"Anna..." began Nils, "do you think the little man with the dog that wasn't there was a goblin?"

Anna stopped trying to open the book and looked down at Nils. Sometimes she forgot how young he was.

"Nils, you know that there aren't any such things as goblins. They're just made up."

"But he had a dog that we couldn't see!"

"Well, that was a bit odd, but we don't really know what we saw, do we?"

"This might be a magic book—a magic, goblin book, and that's why we can't open it. I think we should put it back on the path where we found it and just go home." He was starting to sound a little bit scared.

"No, Nils, we can't leave it here. What if it rains again and the book gets ruined? We'll take it home and see if we can open it there. If it does open, we can see if it has a name or phone number in and we can call that little man and give him his book back. That's the nicest thing to do."

"I don't like it though, Anna. I think it's a goblin book. I think it's dangerous." With that, he snatched the book from his sister's hand and flung it into the dark of the trees by the side of the path.

"NILS!" shouted Anna angrily. "Why did you do that?"

"Because he's a very sensible young man, it seems."

Anna and Nils turned round at the sound of the strange, sandpaper-and-honey voice and saw the little man standing there, holding the lead in one hand, which seemed to be straining with the pull of the dog they couldn't see. Even though they couldn't see the dog, they could hear its low growl.

"Quiet, Dimple," the little man said, tugging at the lead. "I don't think I'll need to let you loose after all. You'll have to wait for some fresh meat."

Anna and Nils looked at each other and then back at the little man. Seeing him up close and still like this, they saw that he was roughly the same height as Nils. He had a back-to-front baseball cap on, with a coil of wiry blonde hair springing out from underneath. He had huge, sparkling, almost amber eyes and skin the colour of—

"Oh, stop staring," said the little man. "I'm not that interesting. You, boy," he continued, tipping his head towards Nils. "Go and find my book, and bring it to me right away. Or I'll let Dimple here have a taste of you."

"Just a minute—" began Anna, not liking the way the little man was speaking to her brother, but the little man just sighed, closed his eyes, raised his eyebrows and held his hand up, indicating for her to be quiet.

"Young lady, I don't have time for any outraged human emotions. I am extremely busy and extremely late. I have an extremely hungry dog here and you and your little friend would make an extremely tasty snack, so I'd advise you just to keep quiet while he gets my book. Off you go," he said, looking back at Nils again.

Nils waited a breath and then scrambled into the trees where he had thrown the book.

Both Anna and the little man followed Nils with their eyes and when they couldn't see him any more, they looked back at each other.

"So," said the little man, "what weather today, hey?"

CHAPTER 4

When Jack Broadsword awoke, he felt different. Changed somehow. He still felt the beat of a warrior's heart in his chest, and the breath of the forest at his neck made him feel alive and at home—but he felt more, somehow. A little more alive, a little more aware of the forest, and the beat of his heart, and the blood in his veins and the feel of the sword in the scabbard by his leg. He felt more... he felt more like a Bengt than a Jack. He stood up with a start and put his hand to his face, and felt the beard there, felt the scar on his cheek where the razor wing had cut deep. Yes, Jack Broadsword, that was his name—pure-hearted warrior of the True Dreamers, hero of the Sapphire Wars, vanquisher of his greatest enemy:

the evil and foul Mandy Musgrave. No, wait, that wasn't right...

He put out a hand to steady himself against the tree. *Doesn't everyone have a favourite tree?* he thought, and then shook his head, wondering where the thought had come from. He looked down and saw a little notebook on the ground with a pen lying across its open pages. Jack bent down and picked it up. His name was written there, in a very ornate manner: *Jack Broadsword*. He also saw some other names he half-recognized—*Oscar Oakheart, William Sky, William Summersky*... He knew them from somewhere, but where? Jack felt a little dizzy. Something was definitely not right with him. He gripped the comforting handle of his sword and breathed out. What witchcraft was this?

CHAPTER 5

Anna could hear her brother in the trees, rustling and cracking and looking for the little man's book. She felt a little scared and a little angry, but she was also more than a little curious.

"Why can't we see your dog?" she blurted out.

"What?" said the little man.

"Your dog. Why can't we see him?"

The little man looked down at the vacant space at the end of his lead, and then at Anna.

"I told you. He's very hungry."

"But that doesn't make any sense." Anna shook her head and held her right wrist with her left hand, which was something she always did when she was stressed or worried. "Just because he's hungry, doesn't mean he's invisible."

The little man sighed, and tugged a little on the lead.

"This is an extremely hungry dog. He hasn't eaten anything for the whole day. He is absolutely vanished."

"Vanished?" echoed Anna. "Don't you mean *famished?*"

"I mean what I mean," snapped the little man. Just then, Nils appeared out of the dark of the woods.

"I-I can't find it," he stammered.

The little man raised his eyes to the heavens and kicked the back of one foot against another.

"Look harder. Oh, and you might try whistling. Something jaunty. That might help."

Nils retreated back into the trees and they could hear his off-key attempt at whistling.

"Beautiful," said the little man, more to himself than to Anna.

"No, but famished means really hungry, and vanished means not there," argued Anna.

"What? Oh, that. It's all a question of letters and words and intent. Say the right words the wrong way, or the wrong words the right way—mean what you say and say what you mean and see what you may. If he's a hungry dog, then it's only a couple of letters changed and he's a vanished dog—and what's a couple of letters between bends?"

Anna was quiet for a moment, then decided to ignore what the little man had said, as she didn't really understand it, and said, "But he's not really vanished, he's not invisible like that—we could see his shadow."

"Of course you could see his shadow!" snapped the little man. "Why wouldn't you see his shadow? It's not like he isn't there. He's just vanished. A good bit of fresh meat..."—Anna didn't like the way he looked at her then—"and he'll be bright as brains again."

"But..." Anna began, but just then Nils hopped out of the woods again with a triumphant smile on his face and the little book held high in his hand.

"Got it!" shouted Nils. "I did what you said. I whistled, and after that I could hear my whistle echoing back in some strange way, and when I followed the echo I found it."

"Yes, well, it likes a good ditty, although it normally likes it to be in tune. Still—okay, very well. My book, please." The little man held out his hand towards Nils.

Nils started to move forward but then hesitated and looked at his sister. She was holding one wrist, which was never a good sign. "Are you a goblin?" he asked, at which the little man snorted.

"Goblin! Do I look like a goblin? Goblins are warty and wobbly and smell of stinky old apples and jimbleberry juice. Do I smell of stinky old apples and jimbleberry juice?"

Nils looked puzzled. "I... I don't know what jimbleberry juice is."

"Ex-stack-lee! If you could smell it, then you'd know it, and you can't, so there you go. No goblin. Book, please." He stretched his hand out even farther, wriggling his fingers.

Nils looked at his sister, who nodded slightly, and then carried on towards the little man, holding the book in front of him. He felt a slight tingle in his fingers as the odd little fellow took the book from him.

"Well, thank you muchly." And with that, he slid the book into the front pocket of his waistcoat.

"Why... why couldn't we open it?" asked Nils, rubbing his hands together to try to get rid of the tingling feeling.

"The book, you mean?" The little man adjusted his baseball cap and scratched his nose. The dog that wasn't there could be heard licking itself a little. "It's not that sort of a book. It's not a book that you open and read, or even the sort of book you open and write in. It's another sort of book."

Anna stepped forward, still gripping her wrist. "What sort?"

"Well, you two are just dripping with questions today, aren't you? And I've already told you that I am extremely late, so I must be on my way." The little man pulled on the lead and started down the path again. Anna stared at him as he walked away, but Nils was staring intently at his fingers, the ones that had handed the book over. He wriggled them a little, blew on them, then stuck his hand out in front of Anna's face.

"Look."

Anna looked at her brother's fingers, and her eyes widened. Scrolling across them seemed to be thousands and thousands of tiny letters and words, like when you whizz through text on a computer screen. She grabbed hold of his wrist and brought his hand closer to her face, so she could really see. After a moment, she looked at Nils.

"This probably isn't good," she said, and Nils gulped.

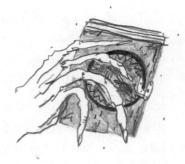

CHAPTER 6

Somewhere else, a smartly dressed man with oil-slick black hair and icicle-bright jellyfish-blue eyes was walking quickly and quietly, keeping to the shadows. In his hands was a very old, very heavy book and in his heart was nothing but greed and a longing for all he'd been promised.

His queen hissed and shivered with pleasure.

Soon. Soon she would be unbound. And then she would make up for all those lost years of steaming frustration, and the horrors within her would run wild once more. She laughed, and it was the sound of thorns scratching at a windowpane on an unfriendly and starless night.

CHAPTER 7

Jack Broadsword strode purposefully through the Darkwood. It was approaching dusk, and he knew it wasn't wise to be here. Nobody should be alone in the Darkwood after sunset, not even a warrior with a hefty steel sword at his hip. He stopped for a second when he thought he heard the howl of the tanglewolves, but they sounded distant, so he thought it was safe to carry on. How long had he been asleep under that tree? And why on earth had he fallen asleep there at all? He had places to be and things to do.

Jack wondered again about the strange little book he had found with his name in it. Where had it come from? Why did those other names seem familiar? Who was this Mandy Musgrave, whose name he had in his head? There was something else scratching at him too—some other impulse or urge or worry tickling the back of his neck and niggling at him. Jack stopped short when it came to him: he mustn't be late home for tea, or his mum would be worried. Jack put the heel of his right hand to his brow and pressed hard against his right eye. He needed to think straight, and he needed to get out of the Darkwood. The tanglewolves were howling again, closer this time.

CHAPTER 8

They had hurried home through Timberton Woods, not seeing the little man again. Maybe he had broken into a run or ducked into the woods themselves—they didn't know, but they were eager to get home, somewhere normal, somewhere that felt safe. Now they were sitting in the small, cosy kitchen. It was a little after four o'clock and no one else was home, so it was only the two of them. Anna had made them some ham sandwiches and hot chocolate, so they were sitting there, leaning over steaming mugs of froth and staring at Nils's left hand.

"Does it hurt?" asked Anna.

"It tingles, but it doesn't hurt. I can almost kind of feel the words and letters tickling across my skin, but that's all it is—more a tickle or a tingle." He looked at Anna. "Is it dangerous, do you think?"

She blinked once, and then smiled kindly at him. She could see that he was scared. "I don't know, Nils. I really don't. But it's good it doesn't hurt."

"Do you think I need to go to the doctor or something?" He bit his lip. Nils hated going to the doctor; he didn't like the way it smelt and all the waiting on the sticky chairs.

"I don't think it's really a doctor kind of thing. It must be to do with the book and the little man. It would be too much of a coincidence otherwise." She reached out and held Nils's wrist, keeping his hand still. "I keep thinking I can read what it says, but then everything moves so fast and I can't."

Nils banged his other hand on the tabletop so hard that the plate of ham sandwiches fell to the floor. "Silly, stupid little man!" he exclaimed.

"Nils!" scolded Anna.

"Sorry," he said quietly. "But I bet he was a goblin, and I bet that was a magic book, and now I've got magic spilled all over my hand and I don't like it. I don't like it at all." And he, very gently, started to cry.

CHAPTER 9

The Darkwood was home to many strange creatures. As long as you kept to the paths and didn't venture in there after the sun set, there was a pretty good chance you wouldn't get to meet any of them, and that would be a good thing. As Jack quickened his pace, with his hand on his sword, he remembered the rhyme they used to sing when he was a child:

> Darkwood dark and Darkwood cold,
> No one knows all the Darkwood holds.
> Little Jimmy Tinderspit wandered on his own,
> Little Jimmy Tinderspit never came home.
> Darkwood dark and Darkwood cold,
> We all know not to be bold.

Sweet Bonnie Applecheeks went to pick cherries,
Now Sweet Bonnie Applecheeks is set to be buried.
Darkwood dark and Darkwood cold,
There are blacker terrors still, yet to be told.

He shivered. Jack knew it was only a rhyme meant to scare children away from somewhere that wasn't safe, but it still resonated with him. He really wanted to be out of the wood and back on the main road, heading for home. Why on earth had he ventured so far into the Darkwood so late in the day? And why had he fallen asleep? His stomach growled a little and again the thought came to him: *Hurry home, you'll be late for tea and Mum will be worried.* Where did that strange thought come from? His parents were long dead. He sighed and looked up at what little of the sky he could see through the treetops—it would soon be night.

Suddenly he heard movement behind him. He whirled round with his hand on his sword and saw a tall, slender man leaning back against a tree. The man's arms were crossed, as were his feet at the ankles. He wore high, scuffed, black leather boots, dark-brown trousers tucked into them, a frock coat of the brightest scarlet, a black T-shirt with a picture of a bat's head and the words *Drink*

Blood on it, and had blue-black hair that reached down to his shoulders. His eyes were bright and lively, and he was smiling at Jack.

"Hiya, Jack. You're out late." He moved his head down and to the left and spat something black and sticky to the ground. "And so are the tanglewolves. Lots of them."

Jack relaxed a little at the sound of the familiar voice, but kept his hand on the hilt of his sword.

"I like your T-shirt, William."

The tall man instinctively looked down at his chest and then back up at Jack. "This? It was on sale, but it is apt, don't you think?" He winked.

Jack nodded, then started walking again. "But, as you say, the tanglewolves are out in force tonight, and I don't want to meet them. I don't think you'd want to either, William."

"Well," said the man, pushing himself away from the tree and following Jack, "You know that the tanglewolves wouldn't bother me, although I suppose they would be a distraction. But..."

William caught up with Jack and put one hand on his shoulder to stop him. He pulled him round slightly to look at him closely.

"Something's changed with you, Jack. What is it? There's something in your eyes, something—"

Before he could finish, Jack knocked the hand away from his shoulder and turned back to his path out of the woods. "Don't touch me, William."

William nodded his head very slightly. "Yes, sorry, I forgot. It still hurts?"

Jack ignored the question and kept his gaze and his stride ahead.

"Jack, wait. I'm sorry, really, I'm sorry. Let me come with you."

Jack was about to reply when the low growl of a tanglewolf broke through the other sounds of the forest. He came to a sudden stop as two yellow eyes and a flash of sharp white teeth burned out of the darkness. "William!" exclaimed Jack, more out of shock than anything else.

But William Wynn was gone. Only Jack and the tanglewolf were left.

CHAPTER 10

Anna stood up, put her arms around her little brother and laid her cheek on the top of his head. She could smell the familiar scent of his favourite Spider-Man shampoo and the leafy smell of Timberton Woods.

"Shh. Shh, Nils. It's all right, it's all right. We can sort it out."

Nils sniffed back a few tears and wiped his eyes with the back of his hand. "When will Mum and Dad be back? They'll know what to do. Won't they?"

Before Anna could answer, there was a loud, insistent banging at the back door of the kitchen. It was less like someone knocking to let you know they were there and more like someone trying to break down the heavy wooden door. Anna instinctively went over to it.

"What?" she snapped, as she pulled the door open.

Standing on the back doorstep was the little man from the woods. He still had the lead in his hand and he didn't look happy.

"Thief!" he shouted, and he pushed his way past her and into the kitchen. "Thieves," he said, when he saw Nils sitting at the kitchen table. "Just a pair of miserable, human, low-life, smelly thieves." And he marched over to where Nils was sitting.

Nils stood up quickly and backed away; they could hear the dog that wasn't there growling.

"You steal my book, throw it into the woods, ask me lots of ignorant, boring, human questions and then you suck the soul out of my book! Ugly, human weasels. Stupid, young thumbjabbers! Blotchy, pink FLESHBAGS! Which one of you smelly brutes has it?"

Now Anna was scared, but she was also becoming quite annoyed. She didn't like that her brother was so scared and was crying. She didn't like that this little man and his dog, that they couldn't see, had scared her in the woods. And she most certainly didn't like that this little man had come into the heart of their home, into a place that was meant to be safe and secure and warm and loving, and begun calling her and her brother horrible names. She especially did not like being called "smelly". Anna followed him into the kitchen and called out: "You just stop right there, mister."

The little man stopped his ranting and looked back over his shoulder at her. "Did the smelly human thief say something?"

Something snapped in Anna, and suddenly she wasn't scared at all any more, or even annoyed. Now she was angry. "OUT!" she yelled, running towards the little man.

The dog that wasn't there growled loudly, and she thought she could even hear teeth snapping, but she just looked down at where the dog ought to have been and yelled again.

"QUIET! You stupid invisible dog. Growl at me and my brother once more, and I'll stick a broomstick up your stupid invisible bottom and use you as a stupid invisible broom!" She didn't even know what that meant, but the dog stopped growling and whimpered a little bit.

"Now, you wait a grape-peeling moment..." began the little man, turning around to look at Anna properly.

"AND YOU!" yelled Anna again. "You are an ugly, badly dressed and rude little man. If there are goblins, and if there are unpleasant ones, then you are the most unpleasant goblin that anybody could ever wish to meet. This is my house and you..." and here Anna surprised herself—and Nils, and the dog that wasn't there, and especially the little man—by reaching down and grabbing the little man by the scruff of his shirt and the back of his trousers, "...are not—"

"HEY! What are you doing? Gerroff!" complained the little man, as he was lifted off the greystone floor, dropping the dog's lead in the process.

"...welcome in my house!" Here, Anna lifted the heavy little man to the door and actually threw him out. Nils's jaw dropped open. "And you stay out!" she yelled, slamming the door.

Outside, the little man called out in pain as he landed in the nearest rose bush.

Inside, Anna looked at Nils, and Nils looked at Anna. Then they both turned towards the sounds of slurping and gulping, as the dog that wasn't there wolfed down the ham sandwiches.

They could both, very clearly, see a disembodied tail wagging in mid-air.

CHAPTER 11

Backing slowly away from the growling shape in the dark, Jack's fingers tightened round the handle of his sword. If the tanglewolf leapt at him, he knew he wouldn't have time to unsheathe it before he felt the creature's ragged, hot breath and cutting teeth. Tanglewolves lived to kill. As he backed away, it moved slowly out of the darkness, its head down low and hackles raised high. Jack could smell the animal now: a rangy, sour-meat smell. This beast was only the scout, searching for prey. Jack knew the rest of the pack would soon be here, and then he would have no chance at all. If he was going to survive, this was his only opportunity to escape.

As he edged back and the tanglewolf prowled forwards, he could more easily make out the wolf's fur standing up on its back, the ears dropped low, the skin around its mouth pulled back to better showcase those sharpsliver teeth, and of course, its tail. The tail was a tanglewolf's most dangerous weapon and what gave them their name. The tail coiled around behind the animal, at least twice as long as the body and head of the wolf itself, moving like an angry, swaying snake. The tail allowed the wolf to hang from branches of trees, to grab prey and squeeze until that prey had no breath left. And when that tail moved fast enough, it could knock a horse to the ground.

Tanglewolves could kill with teeth and tail, savage you in a second from any angle. But that wasn't what was scariest about them. What was scariest was how, suddenly and without warning, a dark, wet mist would start to rise up from the tanglewolf's fur. First you wouldn't be able to see the creature, then you wouldn't be able to see your own hand in front of your face; next the mist would wrap itself greedily around you, and you'd know that in just a heart's breath you'd hear the beast launch itself at you, and you would feel claw or tooth or tail, and the ripping would begin...

That same dark mist was appearing now, steaming up from the silver-grey coat of the wolf and shrouding it, as the shadowbeast edged closer to Jack. The tanglewolf raised its head and howled a song into the nightening sky. The pack, close now, responded with a wild chorus of sharp delight.

Funny, thought Jack, *I never thought it would be a tanglewolf that did for me.* The mist grew thicker and darker all around him.

All at once, there was a beating of wings behind him, above him and around him. The mist fluttered a little and Jack thought he could see something ragged and fast, moving through the air with a high, keening screech of anger. Jack heard the tanglewolf growl again, louder this time, and then the sound of ripping, of tearing flesh, and a splatter of blood landed on his face. He wiped it with the back of his hand, and as the mist cleared he saw the body of the tanglewolf lying motionless on the ground, its throat torn open.

William Wynn was standing over the wolf, buttoning up his so-scarlet frock coat and smirking slightly.

"They certainly are a distraction, these tanglewolves. But the others are closer than I'd like. We should be on our way, Jack, and quickly. Shall we?" He beckoned to the path with one delicate, white hand, as if inviting Jack into a parlour.

"I thought you'd gone," said Jack coldly, moving towards William.

"Did you really think I'd leave you to the mercies of the tanglewolves? On a Wednesday?" William smiled and winked again, a bright blush of beauty in the dark. "And besides, I have a small favour to ask you."

Jack scowled. He was still paying for the last time he'd done William Wynn a favour.

CHAPTER 12

"**Y**ou were awesome," said Nils to Anna, who was standing with her back to the door, gripping one wrist with her hand and shaking very, very slightly. "Like a superhero. Or Granny C when she gets angry with Dad. But..."—he looked over at the wagging tail—"we still have that dog you can't see. Except... except, well, you can see a bit of it now, can't you?"

Anna nodded silently, and looked over to where they could hear the dog happily licking the last morsel from the now empty—and surprisingly clean—plate.

"What are we going to do with it?" asked Nils.

"I..." began Anna, still with her back to the door. She jumped forward with a start as an angry little face banged up against the kitchen window and misted up the glass with hot breath. The little man's baseball hat was missing and he had a few leaves in his hair and a long, thin scratch across one cheek.

"Dimple!" came the slightly muffled voice through the glass. The wagging tail and munching stopped for a moment, then carried on. "You ungrateful mutt!" shouted the little man. "You're anyone's for a sausage, aren't you?"

Both Anna and Nils turned to the window, where the little man had two hands above his head resting on the glass, looking for all the world like a wistful child with their nose pressed up against the toyshop window on Christmas Eve. He closed his eyes and knocked his forehead gently against the windowpane.

"Betrayed for a sausage," he said.

"Ham," said Nils. "They're ham sandwiches."

The little man opened his eyes and sighed, heavily.

Anna and Nils both wondered what they were going to do now, with an unpleasant goblin outside and a quite hungry dog inside, which was gradually becoming more and more visible. This was becoming a most unusual Wednesday.

CHAPTER 13

William Wynn and Jack Broadsword hurried along the path, aware of the sounds of the forest around them. Jack had unsheathed his sword now, and was walking with it in his hand. He still had that strange, uneasy feeling about being late for tea and the name Mandy Musgrave fluttering behind his eyes. The feeling hadn't been there so much when he was facing the tanglewolf, but now it was stronger again.

"If we cut through Kipkorn's Clearing it'd be quicker," said William, looking over at him.

"I want to keep to the path. It shouldn't take long till we're at the village."

William smiled. "You always did like to stick to the rules, Jack."

"And you never obeyed a single rule in your life," replied Jack, not looking at the tall man by his side. "What's this favour you want?"

"Ah," said William, quickening his step to make sure he kept up with Jack, who was now almost jogging. "That. Yes, well. I need you to break the veil with me and help me find a little something that may have got itself very slightly lost."

Jack didn't break his stride, but snorted loudly and gave his walking companion a quick sideways glance. "I don't break the veil."

"There are those pesky rules again that you are so fond of. But look at the treasures you can find..." William gestured towards his T-shirt with the bat on (and now also a splattering of the tanglewolf's blood). "You know that you don't find this sort of finery at the village on market day."

"Rules are there for a reason, William," sighed Jack.

"But just think, my friend—if your parents had stuck to the letter of the law, they would never have taken me in, would they? They couldn't have. Think how dull your life would have been without me around."

"My life, William, without you would have been infinitely better. My mother and father..." And here

Jack stumbled with his words, as once more he had that *bump* inside him about a mother fretting over him being home late, about the safety and security of a home and the wide-open terror of a world full of Mandy Musgraves. As he stumbled over his words, his body too stumbled a little.

"Jack?..." William looked over with concern. "There's something about you today. There's magic in the air, which I suppose isn't that surprising."

The lights of the village could now be seen, glinting softly through the edge of the forest.

Jack composed himself, but William was right: there was something in the air. And there was something about him too. Something *in* him, even.

"I don't break the veil," he repeated, and broke into a run—away from those thoughts, away from William, away from the dark.

CHAPTER 14

By the time the dog that wasn't there had made sure to nearly lick the pattern off the plate and snaffled up every last tiny piece of crumb and crackling from the floor, its tail, hind legs and lower back were visible. It seemed Dimple was an interesting shade of tawny brown, with a very waggy and fluffy tail.

"His tail doesn't look as mean as he sounded when we couldn't see him," said Nils, and Anna nodded in agreement. Leaving the cleanly licked plate behind him, the dog that wasn't entirely there contentedly trotted over to the children and sniffed the air in front of them.

"I think he must still be a bit hungry," said Anna, "as we can't see all of him yet."

Suddenly there was a *rat-a-tat-tat* on the window-pane and the little man called out to them as he knocked on the glass.

"Now you've stolen my book AND my dog. You two humans are a right pair of thieves, aren't you? I'm surprised you're not wearing masks and carrying those guns you lot like so much."

"I didn't want your stupid book," yelled back Nils. "It came off on my fingers. I didn't do anything!"

"Oh no, of course not. Not you—not some butter-tongued thumbjabber. You wouldn't have DREAMT of stealing my book, would you? Just like you wouldn't have tempted my dog with a plate of sausages!"

Nils looked at Anna and said very softly to her, "Why does he keep saying sausages? They were ham sandwiches."

"WHASSAT?" shouted the little man. "What did you say? Jam hand witches? What do you two know about jam hand witches?"

"I think there must be something a little wrong with him," said Nils to Anna. "Unless all goblins are like this. Even the pleasant ones."

"Pheasant buns?" shouted the little man through the glass again. "Don't you dare give Dimple pheasant buns! They'll give him wind and, trust me, you don't want that."

The dog that was starting to be there woofed a very quiet woof and went lolloping over to the door.

"It is his dog," said Anna, "and we don't want it anyway, but I'm afraid of opening the door in case he tries to rush in again." Even though they couldn't see it, they could hear the dog that was halfway there start to paw at the door with his still-famished front leg.

"Good dog, Dimple," called the little man. "No pheasant buns for you today."

Nils was looking at his hand again, at the text spooling across his fingers.

"Maybe he can help us get rid of this silly magic all over my fingers. Maybe we can put it back in his book and he can leave us alone?"

Anna thought for a second or two, then nodded firmly. She walked over to the window and bent down close to the glass so that she could look at the little man nose to nose, and so that he could hear everything she said properly.

"What a huge, human, smelly face you have," said the little man.

"Be quiet," said Anna, "and stop saying that I'm smelly, or else I won't do what I was going to do, which is open the door and let you in so that we can have a civilized, un-rude conversation. We can talk about you getting your dog back and us getting all that writing back in your book of unpleasant goblins." She leant back and folded her arms, looking at the little man.

He was quiet for a few seconds, but then nodded curtly. "Very well. Let me in, then, and I won't mention how much you smell again."

Anna bristled and wagged her finger at him. "Do you want to go in the rose bush again?"

"You caught me by surprise last time. You wouldn't catch me unawares again."

Anna went quiet and stared at him. "Don't test me. It isn't only goblins who can be unpleasant, you know."

"Let me in, then," he repeated, softer this time. And so she did.

CHAPTER 15

Jack liked being in this dark corner of The Shaken Sheep, the smallest and least illuminated inn in the village. He liked the hardwood chair he was sitting on. He liked the feel of it against his back. He liked the old, stained table with the dips and cuts in the wood. He ran one hand over the uneven surface, slowly, feeling the wood rough on his skin. He could feel the faint warmth from the fire reach his cheek. All these things reinforced who he was. Jack Broadsword. Those other, odd whispers faded when he concentrated on reality.

The table was set with a willowing candle, a plate of chickenbread and two tankards of foaming ale. William sat facing him, with his back to the wall, noticing the odd wary look he was getting. Jack tore off a strip of chickenbread to dunk in his ale. William looked at him aghast.

"You're not actually going to dip that in your drink?"

Jack did just that, and then bit into the soggy morsel before staring straight at the disgusted William, who could only shake his head.

"You're an odd man, Jack Broadsword, and there's no mistake."

"Says the man who still has the taste of tangle-wolf blood in his mouth," replied Jack, tearing off another strip of chickenbread.

"Okay, okay," said William, putting up his hands in an attempt to quieten Jack. "No need to tell the world and his uncle." Jack dunked another piece of chickenbread and William looked away.

"I'm not breaking the veil," said Jack, after he had eaten the second piece, sliding the plate towards William, who shook his head and slid it back.

"You say that," said William, pausing to take a mouthful of his ale, "and I can respect you saying that. I can understand why you are saying that, but"—and here he took another sip of his drink—"when you hear what it is that has gone missing, you might change your mind."

There was a rush of colder air through the inn and both men looked to the heavy door as a smallish cloaked figure entered, carrying a wicker basket of dark-crimson mushrooms.

"Bloodshrooms," called the figure, in a hard-to-identify voice, neither man nor woman, boy nor girl. "Freshly picked bloodshrooms, two crowns apiece."

"Now there's a proper snack for a Wednesday. 'Little Saturday' they call it, you know." William smiled and raised his hand. "Here!"

The cloaked figure made his or her way through the inn to the dark corner where the two men were sitting and proffered the basket to them.

"Mmm, how good they look. I think I'll take this one, and that one, and maybe those two..." William helped himself to a selection of the sticky-looking bloodshrooms, before grinning over at Jack and saying, "My friend'll pay."

Jack sighed and reached into the pocket of his jacket for some coins. He counted them over, and the shroom-seller dipped his/her cloaked head and moved away, calling again, "Bloodshrooms! Freshly picked, two crowns apiece."

William had already begun eating the shrooms, and a trickle of red juice was trailing from his mouth. "*Mmgood*," he mumbled.

"I'd offer you one, Jack, but I'm afraid you'd just dunk it."

Jack leant back in his chair and raised his eyes to the smoke- and damp-stained wooden ceiling.

"You never change, William. You still act exactly like the little boy I first met."

William wiped the juice from his chin on his sleeve and winked at Jack.

"Ah, you're only jealous of my boyish charm. That and my supernatural good looks, of course." He chuckled and popped another shroom in his mouth.

Jack shook his head. "Tell me what's gone missing and why it should bother me and why you're looking for it," he said.

William finished chewing and his bright, smiling expression changed. He leant forward, and in a whisper he said: *The Book of All Tomorrow's Dreams.*"

Jack sat up iron-straight and his eyes widened. "But..."

"Exactly," said William, and put another bloodshroom into his mouth.

CHAPTER 16

The little man was sitting on the floor, stroking the head they couldn't see of the dog that wasn't quite there, whose tail was wagging happily.

"Good dog, Dimple," he said softly. "What a good, good dog you are."

Anna and Nils were back sitting at the table, observing the, in its own way, touching scene.

"We didn't actually steal him, you know," said Nils, "and he was only in here on his own for a few minutes."

The little man looked up at Nils with a sad expression on his face. "Shadowdogs and their owners should never get separated. Ever. It's the baddest luck and the worstest feeling." He went back to stroking his dog.

Nils looked at Anna, who shrugged and, after a second, said: "So, can we talk in a civilized way about your book and what's the matter with my brother's hand and who you are, and just everything?"

The little man nodded, finished patting the not-altogether-there dog and stood up. He put his hand to his waist and dipped his head very, very slightly.

"My name is Robert Gribble. Pleased to meet you."

"Robert Gribble!" echoed the children in unison.

"Yes, Robert Gribble. Esquire. Why?" asked the little man—or, apparently, Robert Gribble—looking none too pleased.

"It's just..." started Nils, before trailing off.

"You don't look much like a Robert Gribble," finished Anna, her hand round her mug of hot chocolate (which was now more *medium* chocolate).

"Oh," said the little man, pulling himself up to his full height. "And extractly how is a Robert Gribble supposed to look?"

Nils and Anna looked at each other again, and then back at the little man.

"Well, less like a goblin," said Anna.

"Yes," jumped in Nils, "you look much more like that name on your book. Gribblebob."

"Ah, yes. Well, yes—you see..." The little man started to get flustered and pulled at the neck of his shirt with one hand and adjusted his retrieved baseball cap with the other. "Well, Gribblebob is sort of my name too, but, uh, I don't use it here, you see. No, here it is Robert Gribble. Just plain, simple Robert Gribble. It's in the phone book and everything."

"What's a phone book?" asked Nils.

"They had them in the olden days," said Anna, "before the internet."

"I like phone books," muttered the little man. "You know where you are with a phone book."

Anna looked like she was contemplating something, which in fact she was.

"When you say 'here', what do you mean? Do you mean 'here' as in Uppington Down, or 'here' as in Sussex or England or the United Kingdom or Europe or... or what?"

There was a slight pause, and the little man bent down to start patting the unseen head of his dog once more. From the sound of it, the dog licked the little man's hand.

"Hmm. Well, I suppose if we're going to talk about my book and your hand then you need to know, but I'm still not sure if it's a good idea."

"What?" asked Nils, looking very confused indeed.

The little man made a deep sigh, took off his baseball cap, smoothed his hair and put the cap back on again.

"This side of the veil I am Robert Gribble, Esquire, normal, run-of-the-mill person about town, but on the other side of the veil I am Gribblebob," he paused a beat, "goblin."

"Unpleasant?" questioned Anna.

The little man's eyes narrowed. "When necessary, very."

There was a moment's silence as that sunk in, then Anna asked: "What do you mean 'the veil'? This side of the veil, that side of the veil—what does that mean?"

The little man sighed and seemed to ruffle the back of the neck of the not-all-there dog. "Do you believe in goblins and fairies and dragons and all that malarkey?"

"No," replied Anna and "Yes," said Nils, both at the same time. They looked at each other and grinned.

"Well, I'm starting to believe a bit more after today," Anna added, and the little man nodded.

"Yes, well, that's very typical of your lot; you can't take something on faith, you have to see it for yourself before you know it to be true. But then you spend so much time looking down at your thumbjabbering machines that you never see anything for yourself anyway. You're too busy looking through someone else's window. And how often is that cleaned, hmm?"

Anna and Nils didn't really get what he meant, so they stayed quiet. The little man shrugged and carried on.

"So, let me tell you. Let me make it clear. I am a goblin, and my name is Gribblebob. This is my shadowdog, Dimple. However, I live here in your village, and here I'm Robert Gribble of Webstone Cottage, Blacksmith's Lane. I've lived here about three years now. Kept myself to myself. Not made a fuss. I buy the odd pint of ale, read the local paper, watch your footyball on the television and enjoy everything being so, so, well... ungobliny, if you see what I mean."

"No," said Nils, and Anna shook her head.

"I say I've lived here about three years, and that's true. But it's also true to say that I've lived here all my life, and that's a very long time. Isn't it, Dimple?" He played with the fully invisible ears of his partly invisible dog.

"You're not really being very clear," said Anna.

"Hmm. Well, okay. Let's see, then. Here, where we are now... this village, this house, this floor" and he stamped loudly on the floor with one little foot, making them all jump, "is all very solid and real. But there's more to a tree than what you see."

He looked at them knowingly.

"Um, you're still not being very clear," Anna said quietly.

"A tree. You look at a tree and you see this big piece of wood sticking out of the ground. That's what you see. But you don't see the roots, do you? Oh, sometimes bumpy bits stick up and you trip up on them, but most times you don't see the roots, even though they're there. And the leaves reaching up, reaching out. Do you really look at them? Do you sit and watch them change colour? Do you see where the tree meets the sky? Where the tree reaches deep into the soil? Do you see the rings of the tree? All those years? Do you heck-as-like!"

Nils and Anna looked at him in silence again, so he sighed and carried on.

"This place"—and he stamped again—"is like a tree. You see what you see. But you don't see any more. You don't see the roots of your world. You don't see all those hundreds and hundreds of years that have passed. All those years of stories and fables and tales and secrets. You don't see where your world touches the sky and hides the deeper meanings. If you follow the roots, if you see the years, if you touch the sky... then you find yourself somewhere else. The world within your world. The world of goblins and fairies and dragons and all those things that you think are only stories. That's my world. That's where I come from. It's the world that your world is built upon. Here, but not here. Real, but not real. Seen, but not seen."

"A bit like your dog!" jumped in Nils, smiling.

"No," said the little man, looking puzzled.

"So if that's your world, why are you here?" Anna asked quickly.

"Got tired of it all. Fairies are blooming boring after a while. Dragon poo all over the place. Magic this and magic that... I like it here. Not too keen on you lot, which is why I keep my distance, but I like how different it is from my world."

"You still haven't explained about the veil," said Nils.

"Ah, yes, the veil. Well, that's what we call it, the wall between this world and my world. There are certain places you can break through, where you can cross from one world to the other. You just have to know where they are and what to do. And that's called 'breaking the veil', not that you're really meant to, but—"

"Show us," interrupted Anna.

"Show you?!" snorted the little man.

"Yes, show us, so we'll know it's all true."

Nils put his hand up. "Um. What about my hand?"

"Oh. I'd forgotten about that," said Anna. "Sorry, Nils."

Nils harrumphed.

CHAPTER 17

William wiped the last drop of bloodshroom juice from his lips and sat back in his chair.

"So now you know why I need you to cross the veil with me."

Jack had been sitting in stunned silence, but now he leant forward and looked very intently into William's eyes.

"But... that's impossible."

"What? Crossing the veil with me, or *The Book of All Tomorrow's Dreams* going missing?" William smiled.

"Both."

William simply carried on smiling and waited for Jack to continue.

"What makes you so sure that the book has been taken across the veil?" Jack finally asked.

"You know me, Jack. I have sources. I have contacts. I know people. People tell me things. People trust me."

"Only fools trust you, William Wynn. As I well know."

Jack gave William a particularly meaningful glare as he said this, and William's face lost its almost permanent look of gentle amusement. He lowered his eyes and scratched his cheek, just below his right eye, with a long fingernail.

"Hmm," was all William said, before he recovered his composure and looked back up at Jack with a grin. "Well, that's as maybe. But the fact is that people do tell me things, and I happen to know that the book has been taken 'cross the veil. And I have an idea where it might be, and why it might be there, and who it might be with. And I also have an idea that if I—if we—can find the book and return it to where it belongs, there will be tremendous benefits for us. For both of us."

"But mainly for you, I'd wager."

William's smile retreated once more.

"I have debts I need to pay, Jack, you know that. I need your help. I can't get the book back without you. And you know how dangerous it could be if the book gets into the wrong hands. There have been signs already. You've noticed. I can tell."

Jack thought of the strange thoughts he'd been having since he woke up under the tree. Late for tea. Mandy Musgrave. Oscar Oakheart.

"Can you now?"

"I know you, Jack. I know you better than I know anyone."

"And I know you, William Wynn. Don't forget that. I know you. I know the little boy who came into my home and charmed my parents with his smile and his laugh and his pretty tricks."

William's face clouded slightly. "And you, Jack, didn't I charm you too?"

"Yes, and me, of course."

"We had fun, didn't we, when we were small?" Jack said nothing.

"So, you see," said William sharply, snapping back to the matter at hand. "The book has to be found. You and me, Jack. Like old times. Like—"

"Those times are gone, William. Those times ended that day in the Stormlands when you left me with a dovestone arrowhead in my shoulder, a swarmwind bearing down on me and a long walk home."

William's smile vanished altogether, and there was real hurt in his eyes.

"You know why, Jack. My sister. It was a chance to find my sister."

"And wasn't I all but your brother, William?"

There was a moment of silence long enough for a bright glitter of tears to be seen forming in William's eyes. And then he replied. "Of course. Always."

Jack shook his head. "That dog has howled, William, but getting the book back is important, for everybody. So I'll help you. But it isn't going to be like old times."

William blinked away the tears and nodded. "Then let's go."

CHAPTER 18

Nils, Anna, Dimple and Gribblebob—or Robert Gribble, depending on how you looked at it—were making their way back past Timberton Woods, towards the park. They had agreed that before doing anything about Nils's hand, the little man would show them the other side of the veil. He needed to fetch something from the other side anyway, he said, to help with getting all the magic back into the book from Nils's hand.

"How long will it take?" asked Nils, as they walked along the path. "Won't Mum and Dad be worried?"

Anna shook her head. "Remember, they were both going over to Uncle Oscar's after work, to help him put all that new flat-pack furniture together."

"Oh yeah," said Nils, remembering the break-down Uncle Oscar had over a rocking chair that ended up rocking side to side rather than back and forth. "He never has much luck with those sorts of things, does he?"

"Anyway," continued Anna, "they said they were going to have a takeaway together afterwards and wouldn't be back until late, so we were going to get our own tea tonight. But I've left them a note on the fridge to say we've gone back to the park for a bit, just in case they come home early."

"Very antique," said Gribblebob. "I thought you lot all had your thumbjabbering machines to leave each other vexed messages and M&Ms."

"M&Ms?" questioned Anna. "You mean the sweet?"

"Huh?" said Gribblebob, his wild eyebrows shooting up to his baseball cap. "I suppose they could be sweet. Depends what they're of, I s'pose."

"I think he means MMSs," said Nils, "on the phone."

"Oh," said Anna. "You mean MMS, picture messages?"

"That's exactly what I said," the little man replied huffily. "M&Ms. Now..." He stopped walk-ing and the two children and the dog all stopped too. He lowered his voice and carried on speaking. "When we get there, you need to do exactly what I say, when I say it. And you might find that you feel a bit dizzy and woozy once we've gone through the veil. That's quite normal, don't panic. I know that you lot tend to panic, so don't."

"So where exactly is it we're going?" asked Anna. "The playground in the park?"

"Not exactly. In fact, we're nearly there. Look." Gribblebob pointed over to the wooden outdoor gym area, right in the far corner of the park.

"The gym?" said Nils in surprise. "We get through to the other side from the gym?"

"That climbing frame thingy," Gribblebob said. "On this side of the veil it looks like that, but it looks quite different on the other side. And that's where we're going."

"But why aren't people falling into the other side all the time if it's just through the climbing frame?" Anna asked.

Gribblebob tapped the side of his slightly hairy nose with one stumpy finger and said, in a low voice, "Reasons."

"What sort of reasons?" Anna responded, as the little man started marching towards the corner of the park, Nils and Anna hurrying with him.

"It's like a puzzle. If you know what pieces you're looking for, and if you know how to fit them together, then the puzzle's puzzled and Jack's your beansprout. If you don't even know there's a puzzle there, then you don't see it and you never puzzle it. You'll see when I show you. Oh." And the little man suddenly stopped walking again. "One thing. When I said that you're not really meant to break the veil—well, you're really, really not meant to break the veil. In fact, on the other side, it's kind of against the law, and it's especially against the law for people like me to bring people like you from this side to that side. Very against the law, in fact."

He was quiet. The children waited for him to continue talking, but instead he just started walking again. Anna and Nils started after him.

"Wait," said Anna. "What then? Are we not going through after all?"

"Oh no, we're going through. I said I'd show you, and I need... that thing... to help get all the magic back in my book. But if we do get caught, it's everyone for themselves."

"What does that mean?" gulped Nils.

"It means that I'll swear on my brother's knife that I never met hide nor hair of you before and you'll have to answer to the Court of Naughtiness yourself."

Anna and Nils both broke out laughing. "The Court of Naughtiness?" giggled Anna. "That doesn't sound at all scary. It sounds like something at a nursery school. What do they do? Put you on the naughty step for thirty minutes and stop you having your afternoon milk?"

Gribblebob stopped again and turned to the children with an extremely serious expression on his face.

"You may well think the Court of Naughtiness sounds funny. But I can on-shore you that it won't be particularly funny when they carve you into statues and plant you in the Stone Field." And with that, he was off again, leaving the children open-mouthed and slightly more nervous than they had been before.

CHAPTER 19

William and Jack were walking at a brisk pace through the village of Downington Upp. The moon had come up and it was a fine night. William drew many admiring glances from the villagers as they passed, and he smiled and made little half-bows as they went.

"I see you've lost none of your charm," scowled Jack.

"Oh, come. You know they can't help themselves. It's my nature."

Jack let out a loud hoot of derision and they carried on to the outskirts of the village. They were heading to the Blew Stones: seventeen huge blue boulders that, legend had it, had been blown from the Stormlands by an angry ogre in ancient times

74

and had landed in the random tumble they now occupied; some lying on top of others, some resting lengthways against each other, two of them sunk halfway down into the mossy ground. The moonlight was catching them well this evening and they seemed to radiate a soft, shimmering azure blue.

"It's a good night for it," said William, smiling.

"It's a good, bright night for getting caught, you mean," replied a stern-faced Jack.

"Ah, you see, Jack—it is just like old times after all. You with your never-ending optimism and me with, well, this face."

Jack looked over at William and, for once, could not stop a very small smile touching the corners of his mouth. Despite himself, despite all that had happened, he felt a warmth for William that could never really cool. They had grown up together from when they were both seven years old. William's parents had been killed in the Great Uprising and Jack's father had found William crying and shaking uncontrollably by the edge of the Ruining River, his older sister nowhere to be found. The laws at that time were that shadowfolk had to live with their own kind. But there had been something in the need and desperation of that young boy's face that outshone the darkness and ignorance of those ugly and shameful rules, and Jack's father had gathered the trembling boy in his arms and carried him away from the river, carried him home, carried him right into the family. Yes, William was family. Despite it all.

William noticed the small smile on Jack's lips, and couldn't stop himself from giving a full-force, beaming smile back. Luckily, he was able to bite his tongue and stop himself saying anything that might have damaged the moment. It had been such a long time since they had spent time together, had really spoken to one another.

As they approached the Blew Stones, Jack looked back over his shoulder to see if anyone from the village had followed them. He knew that William had the knack of attracting followers, but thankfully tonight no one was behind them.

"It's been a very long time since I pierced the veil," said Jack.

"Whereas I still have the soil from the other side on my boots," noted William, "so let me lead the way."

William went to the largest of the big, glimmering stones, one of the two that had sunk down into the earth, and placed his hand in a barely visible indent in its surface. He pushed his palm hard against the stone, feeling it cold against his skin, then pushed farther, so that his hand actually moved into the rock itself, into the space that lay just beyond the surface. He pushed again, so that his arm was as far in as his elbow. He moved his fingers around inside the empty space he couldn't see, until he felt the tips of his fingers graze a knobble of something like hardening clay. Pushing forward a little more so that his fingers could grab a handful of the substance, he closed his hand tight around it and pulled his arm out.

"Got it!" he said in triumph.

Then he went to the smallest stone, one that lay across two upright stones like a gateway, on the other side of the large stone. With the hand that didn't have a fistful of the Blew Stone innards, he stroked the surface of the stone until he found what he was looking for: a very small dip, right at the top. He moved his other hand above the dip and unclenched his fist so the drippy slime-like stuff fell into the indent. It was dark, deep-sea blue, with odd little sparkles and specks of stony silver. He patted it down smooth. As he did so, there seemed to be some sort of thrumming noise coming from the three gateway stones, and the blue glimmer in them seemed to intensify.

"Come now," said William. "That was quite a big handful, so we should both have time to get through." Jack nodded as William bent low and walked through the gateway. As he did, the thrumming noise grew louder, and there was a clay-slurping noise, and all of a sudden he wasn't there any more.

Jack swallowed. Now it was his turn.

CHAPTER 20

"**W**hen you say 'carve', do you actually mean it or is that just an expression?" asked Anna as they caught up to the little man, who was now standing in front of the climbing frame.

"What?" he snapped. "Oh, never mind that now." He looked around. "It's getting later and it's not as bright as it was—that's good. We don't want too many people around. You lot tend not to notice too much of what goes on around you—what *really* goes on around you—but it's still better to be flat than fluffy."

Nils looked at Anna questioningly, but she just shrugged.

Gribblebob was running his hand over the smooth wood of one of the upright beams of the frame. "Now, then," he said, "I just need to try and find the—"

"What's that noise?" asked Nils. Indeed, there was a low, strange, sour noise in the air, like a slightly out-of-rhythm drum beat, gradually becoming louder.

"Well, that's unexpected," muttered Gribblebob, and moved back from the frame.

As he did, and the children instinctively stepped back too, the whole climbing frame seemed to shimmer slightly, and go slightly out of focus, before the strange noise stopped and the frame came back into sharp relief. What also came into sharp relief was a tall, strange man in a bright-red frock coat, who was now stood right in the middle of the frame. He seemed to stagger slightly, before putting his hand on one of the climbing frame beams to steady himself. The dog that was halfway there barked once, Gribblebob sighed and kicked at the ground with a tetchy foot, and the children looked at each other open-mouthed.

The tall man shook his head slightly, and stood up straight, noticing his audience for the first time. For just a few seconds he looked a little shaken, but then he made a very courteous bow, one hand at his waist, and gave a warm smile that put both

Anna and Nils at ease, despite the fact that this very odd man had seemingly just appeared out of nowhere—well, actually out of the middle of a council climbing frame.

Everyone stood there in silence for a second or two, before Nils very bravely said: "I... I like your T-shirt. My Uncle Oscar has got one just like it."

"In that case," said the strange man, in a voice of honey chocolate, "I think I would have to say that your Uncle Oscar sounds like a very stylish fellow indeed."

Before Nils could say anything else, that same sour noise started again, and the climbing frame started to shimmer.

CHAPTER 21

Jack always hated the feeling of breaking the veil. Stepping through was like having a cold shower from the inside out, and when you got to the other side it always felt like you had stood up too quickly and your head was thick and swimmy. Which was exactly how he was feeling now. He felt himself wobble a bit, then his head cleared and his eyes adjusted to where he now found himself. Which was looking at William talking to two children from this side of the veil and a goblin. A goblin in a very odd hat.

"How many of you are there?" he heard the boy ask, and William looked over his shoulder and winked at Jack.

"I can safely say there is only room for one of me in any world, and possibly only one of him too."

"So no more of you are going to pop out then?" asked the boy.

"Well, it would be a surprise."

As Jack walked forwards, he felt himself wobble again. It was always unsettling to break the veil, but it was different this time. He felt woozy, but as well as that it almost felt like coming home. Which was very strange. The whisperings at the back of his eyes, the odd names and feelings— Mandy, Oakheart, Summersky, late for tea—they were all louder and stronger again, despite how hard he tried to push them down. There was something else too, something new. Like something, somebody even, was stirring inside him, stretching awake. A name came swirling towards him, blown like a memory from a long-ago dream: *Bengt.*

"Jack?..." William called out. "Are you alright?"

"I-I'm fine," said Jack, pulling himself together. "William. What's going on?"

"That," said Gribblebob, before William could answer, "is ecstatically what I would like to know. What is going on?"

"Don't I know you?" Jack asked, looking down at the little man as he ducked his head and stepped out of the climbing frame. "Ah yes, you're that goblin who lost his appetite for magic. What was your name again? Bobblehead, or something?"

The children snorted, Dimple barked and the little man shot them a glance that would have wilted walnuts. "Gribble... bob," he enunciated.

Nils put his hand to his mouth and whispered to Anna, "I think I prefer Bobblehead."

They both laughed again.

"Yes, well. We can't stand here chatting," said Jack to the little group. "We have places to be, don't we, William?" As he said this, he glanced over at his fellow veil-breaker, who nodded.

"Hang on a halfpenny," said Gribblebob sternly. "What are you two tall louts doing breaking the veil? What are you up to?"

"Absolutely nothing to do with you, and—" Jack's sentence was interrupted by Nils, who let out a loud "Hey!" as William suddenly grabbed his wrist and pulled him towards him, looking intently at the boy's hand with the text scrolling over it. His smile had vanished.

"And what's happened here, my young friend?" William asked quietly. Nils looked over at Anna, who then looked at Gribblebob, who looked up at the sky, whistled and walked over to where William was turning Nils's left hand over and over in his own.

"He had a bit of bother with my book. Ended up with it all over his hand. Blurry nuisance. Got to sort it out."

William looked over quietly at Jack, who was approaching them now.

"Not a good week for books, Jack, from the look of things."

"What book?" asked Jack, looking down at Nils's hand and the spooling characters. Gribblebob said nothing, and after a moment Anna spoke up.

"It was called *Gribblebob's Book of Unpleasant Goblins and... other something something*, I think. And we were going to break the veil to sort things out and get it all out of my brother's hand."

Jack arched an eyebrow. "Oh. So you were going to break the veil, were you?" He looked over at Gribblebob, who was studying his feet, and addressed him directly. "And what made you think it was a good idea to take two young ones from this side to our side?"

"I needs my book back in its right and proper."

William let go of Nils's hand. "Well, that's a feeling we can get behind. Isn't that right, Jack?"

Jack sighed. "Come on, we need to go somewhere not quite so conspicuous."

85

"But we need to break the veil," objected Anna, "and help my brother."

"I'm afraid there'll be no breaking of the veil for you today, young miss," said Jack, and Anna bristled.

"And who suddenly went and put you in charge," she answered back, surprising herself slightly, "some strange man who popped out of a climbing frame?"

Jack stared at her for a moment, and there was a stirring inside him. He knew this girl from somewhere. From that wide-open world of terror. He shook his head sharply to shake it all away, then bowed slightly to her. "My apologies. There have been no proper introductions."

"Apart from Bobblehead," corrected William, smiling.

"Oi! Manners," grumbled the little man.

"My name is B-B..." Jack stuttered, and William shot him a worried look. "...Jack Broadsword," he continued. "This is my... this is William Wynn, and it would seem the friendly fates have indeed conspired to place we two in charge. So, might I now enquire the names of this fine young fellow and fair young lady?"

Anna glared in silence at Jack as he stood there waiting for a reply.

"Do you know," she finally said, "Jack Broadsword sounds very much like a made-up name."

And, deep inside him, Jack had a feeling she was right.

CHAPTER 22

All five of them—apart from Dimple, who was tied up outside—were sitting in The Tartan Teapot, one of two tea shops in the village, which was run by a rather temperamental old gentleman from Scotland named Mr Frasier McCurdey and his long-suffering daughter, Isla. The other tea shop, Pippa's Pantry, still closed at quarter to four, but recently Mr McCurdey had started late-night openings on Mondays, Wednesdays and Fridays. *Never too late for tea, toast and tarts!* was the slogan, very ornately written in blue and red chalk on the blackboard by the door.

The group were an odd sight, sitting round a daintily laid table: the little man with his shock of hair and baseball cap, Nils trying to keep his left hand hidden, William with his megawatt smile and red frock coat, Anna with her barely concealed fury, and of course Jack with his huge sword by his side, which was now resting at a strange angle on the wooden floor. The Tartan Teapot didn't often get customers like this. When they had entered the establishment, Frasier McCurdey had taken one look at Jack's sword and moved with astonishing speed to block his entrance.

"Is that a sword?" he had asked, nodding at the sword. Jack had followed his gaze to what was, without question, a sword hanging by his side, and nodded affirmatively.

"Yes, it's a sword."

"Don't get many swords round here."

"No. I suppose not."

"Why do you think you need a sword in my tea shop? We do have cake slices on the premises. Good ones."

"I'm sure you do."

"I'm not licensed for swords."

"Ah-ha."

"I suppose I could charge you swordage—"

William, who could see that this conversation was heading towards a disappointing conclusion, interrupted them. "My friend and I are performers, street performers. That is only a prop, nothing more. It won't cause any damage, I assure you."

Isla McCurdey had just then come out of the back—carrying a plate of welsh rarebit for old Mr Broadchip, who was the only other customer, sitting by the window doing a crossword, his hearing aid turned up much too high, as usual—and she had seen her father talking to these two strange men, one of whom seemed to be wearing a sword and the other who looked like a rock star.

"All okay, Dad?" she had asked, putting the welsh rarebit down by Mr Broadchip, who had started slightly at the noise, and then she had seen Nils and Anna behind the two tall men. "Oh, hello, you two," she said. "Table for four, is it?"

"Five," stated Gribblebob sourly, poking his head out from behind the children. Isla had jumped a little.

"Sorry, of course—five."

"And *he* better not have a sword either, not even a little one," said her father.

"Dad!" Isla had admonished. "Hadn't you better be getting on with the leek and potato soup?"

And so now the five of them were sitting round the table drinking blackcurrant cordial, eating ginger-snap biscuits and talking in very, very soft voices.

"Why did we have to come into this tatty tartan tea shop?" grumbled Gribblebob. "The owner's a buffaloon."

"We couldn't very well stand around by the climbing frame all night, looking odd and suspicious," said Anna.

"No, so we'll just sit here; one goblin, one boy with a stolen magic book on his hand, one angry girl, one sword-waving tub of muscle, and whatever on earth that is"—he jerked his head in the direction of William—"all squeezed in around a tiny tartan table having afternoon tea, like some type of knitting circle, looking not at all odd and not at all suspicious."

"Is he always like this?" asked William to Nils quietly.

"We only met him today... but, yes, he does seem to be like this most of the time," whispered Nils.

"Who's 'he'?" asked Gribblebob. "The cat's brother?" He attempted to dunk his ginger snap in his glass of blackcurrant cordial.

"Eww," said Nils, as the biscuit dissolved into a biscuity mess in the glass.

"Typical!" snapped the little man. "Even the biscuits don't work in this dumpling."

"Please!" said Anna, really quite loudly, so that it rang like a fire siren in Mr Broadchip's hearing aid and he dropped his welsh rarebit. "Can't we talk about serious things? We need to fix Nils's hand, we need to know why you won't let us break the veil and I'd like to know what you two are doing here with made-up names and weird weapons."

Jack nodded.

"You're right. There are things to talk about. I don't think it's a coincidence that you three have had some trouble with a book at the same time we're having some trouble with a book."

"Another magic book?" asked Nils.

William and Jack shared a moment's look, and Jack gave a barely noticeable nod to William, who sat upright and took over the conversation.

"Yes. Another magic book. But this one's a really very important book."

"Oi!" interjected the goblin. "Bitter respect, please."

"Shh!" said Anna, holding a slender finger to her lips.

Gribblebob shrugged and muttered under his breath: "'*This* one's important'. Muddy cheek!"

Anna glared at him and he shut up.

"Really very important indeed," continued William. "You see, a long time ago, on our side of the veil, we had a... problem. With the Rider." The way he said it, and paused, made it seem like he expected to be understood, but Anna shook her head slightly and repeated:

"The Rider?..."

"Yes, the..." William paused again and sighed. He looked at Anna and held her gaze for a few long seconds. Anna blushed a little. "Have you ever had a nightmare?" he asked.

"Of course," she replied, with a quizzical expression. "Everyone has."

"No, I'm not talking about just a bad dream, or a sad dream or some such. I'm talking about a real, howling, ripping nightmare, where you wake up screaming and your hair is slick with sweat and your heart is pumping like a piston, and the terror from your sleep is still with you, on you, in you. Have you ever had something like that?"

"I..." began Anna. "No, no. Not like that."

"No, good. Well, a long time ago, where I come from, there were a lot of nightmares, more than is in any way normal. People of all ages, all types, were affected—goblins, humans, whoever. Some people woke up screaming and were never the same. Some people never woke up." He paused and lowered his head. "It was a dark time."

"So... why?" asked Anna. "What was causing it all?"

"The Rider," said William, looking up again.

"Or Mare, or Mara, or Maya," put in Jack. "She goes by many names."

"I don't get it," said Nils very softly. "Who... what is she? What does she do?"

"Nobody quite knows," went on William, "but whatever she is, she's very old. She goes back to before the veil was put up between our worlds, back when we were one."

"What?" said Anna, in real surprise.

"Long story. Old news," muttered Gribblebob. "Another day."

"But... what did she do?" asked Nils again.

"When she came, she came at night. In the deadest, blackest part of the night. She came into your room, when you were in your deepest sleep. She knelt down by your bed and placed her head next to yours. Sometimes her long hair would fall across your face and you would stir slightly. She listened to your breathing, watched your chest move up and down, and she placed her long, thin fingers just so, so lightly on your eyelids, so that she could feel your eyes flutter beneath the skin. She got a taste of your dreams. Sometimes, if she didn't like the taste, she'd move on. Most times, normally. But if she liked the taste, if she got the right scent, then she'd choose you." William paused again, looking down at his boots.

"Choose you? What do you mean?" asked Anna.

"She'd choose to ride your dreams. She'd jump on your chest, straddling you, one leg either side. She would reach down and her hair would fall over your face, she would put one hand on each ear, and then she would taste your dreams deeply, breathing in their scent, seeing what it was you saw. But as she took your dreams, she would give you what was inside her, turned this way and that way to muddle up with your own thoughts. And what's inside her is bad. Evil. Terrible. The more of your dream she took, the worse your nightmare became. Something awful. Then, when you were shaking and whimpering and crying and sniffling, she'd leave you, leave you with the nightmare left on your cheek... and you'd wake up."

"If you were lucky," added Gribblebob.

"If you were lucky," echoed William, looking over at the little man.

Nils shivered.

"That's horrible," said Anna.

"That's Mara," said Jack. "That's the Rider."

"But, but..." said Nils, looking truly scared. "You said that was then... She doesn't come now, does she?"

"Well..."

"Soup's ready!" shouted Frasier McCurdey proudly from the kitchen, and Mr Broadchip dropped his welsh rarebit again, as his hearing aid vibrated with a Scottish accent.

CHAPTER 23

"She's still out there. She comes, she listens, she might ride your dreams, but the nightmares no longer come in the same way," went on William. "She's not as strong as she was, and that is where the book comes in."

"Yes, the really important book. Tell them about the 'really important' book," muttered Gribblebob.

"Well, the Rider, Mara," said William, "was becoming more and more powerful. She was gaining power from all the dreams she rode. There were more and more nightmares, and the nightmares were becoming worse and worse. People were afraid to sleep, afraid of what they might dream—"

"Afraid that they wouldn't wake up," interrupted Jack.

"Yes, that too," continued William. "So something had to be done. And it was. Everyone came together, everyone pooled their magic—magicians, seers, wizards, witches—"

"Goblins," interjected the goblin.

"Goblins." William nodded. "And a great spell was cast. A protective spell. I don't think a greater spell has ever been cast. It reached over the land, over time, even through the veil—because by this time the veil had come down. This spell laid a thin layer of mist over all the dreams to come, all the dreams not yet dreamt. It meant that even though Mara could still try and ride your dreams, she couldn't quite get the taste, the scent, of them. So the nightmare plague stopped. She was very angry. There were a lot of bad and sad dreams for a while, but no nightmares."

"But what about the book, then?" asked Nils.

"The spell needed a vessel—something to hold it, something to keep it safe. Something powerful. Books are powerful. Books are probably one of the most powerful things people ever hold in their hands, without realizing it. The spell to protect all those future dreams was bound in a book, and that book was hidden somewhere. They say Mara has spent hundreds and hundreds of years searching for the book, to destroy it, to break the spell that keeps her weak." William sat back in his chair and took a sip of blackcurrant cordial, staining his lips dark blue.

"Um..." said Anna, touching her finger to her lips.

"Oh, sorry," said William and licked his lips clean.

Jack tsked, shook his head and took up the story. "It's called *The Book of All Tomorrow's Dreams*, and only a handful of people from one generation to the next know its hiding place. As William said, Mara has been wandering the world searching for it, and she has helpers too now, rip-riders they call them. It seems the book has very recently gone missing from its hiding place, and William here has an idea it has been taken to this side of the veil. So we are trying to find it and return it, and hope the Rider doesn't get her hands on it first."

"How do you know she wasn't the one who took it?" asked Anna. "How do you know she doesn't have it now?"

"I think we'd know if she had it," answered Jack. "But something's afoot. There's magic in the air, the dreamworld is not as it should be, there are... stirrings..." His voice trailed off as once more he felt something, someone even, deep inside him, struggling to come to the surface. There was that name again, ringing in him, louder and louder: *Bengt, Bengt, Bengt.*

"You said something about... rip-riders?" said Anna, and Gribblebob shivered.

"Ah, yes, rip-riders," Jack said, snapping back to the here and now, pushing the ringing name away. "Well, when Mara was at her most powerful, when the nightmare plague was night after night after night, there were many people who didn't wake up in the morning. They stayed alive only within their nightmare. Can you imagine how awful that must be, living only in Mara's world? The sole comfort they take is from Mara herself. If the rip-riders do her bidding, if they keep Mara happy, then she softens their nightmare, makes their unending torment slightly easier to bear."

"It's horrible," said Anna, shaken.

"And the rip-riders are dangerous," said William. "Unlike Mara, who is only a creature of sleep and dreams and the dark, those poor souls who became rip-riders were just like you and me. Well," and he directed his full beamforce smile at Anna, "like you, anyway. And because they once lived in the light, walked the world, the rip-riders can ride people anytime, day or night, dark or light."

"You mean ride people's dreams, like Mara, and give them nightmares, even when they aren't asleep?" asked Anna.

"No, sorry, no. Not like that. I mean that the rip-riders, who now exist as... wraiths, spirits, ghosts—call them what you will—they can settle on anyone, rip into them, ride them. Possess them, I suppose you might say. Make them do whatever Mara wants. And they're powerful, not in the same way as Mara, but they can dip into her magic, tap into her darkness."

"It really is just so horrible, horrible, horrible," repeated Anna.

"But what happens if one gets you?" asked Nils, one hand gripped tight on his glass of cordial. "Can't you do anything to get rid of it? How does it feel when they get you? Does it hurt?"

"Well..." began William.

Just then Frasier McCurdey came over to the table with a little notepad in his hands.

"Will you be wanting anything else?"

"No, I don't think so, Mr McCurdey, thank you," replied Anna, keen to return to the conversation they had been having.

"We have soup now. Leek and potato."

"No, honestly, I think we're all fine," she said again.

"Homemade. Not any of that tinned rubbish you get at Pippa's Pantry."

Anna shook her head and forced the most polite smile she could manage in the circumstances.

"It comes with a roll and butter." He glared over at Jack. "And we have bread knives."

Jack sipped his cordial quietly.

"Sharp ones," he went on.

"No, thank you. Nothing more. Thank you," said Anna, still smiling.

"So you'll be wanting your bill then? Be wanting to get on your way? Before the late-night rush starts?"

"Well, we thought we'd finish our biscuits first." Anna waved a ginger snap at Mr McCurdey as politely as it is possible to wave a ginger snap at anyone.

The tea shop owner snorted and turned back towards the kitchen, where Isla was smiling at William, who in turn was beaming back at her. Nils could hear the café owner mumbling under his breath as he moved away.

"*Pippa's* pigging *Pantry.*"

"He reminds me a bit of you," Nils said to Gribblebob very quietly.

"HIM?" spluttered the goblin loudly, and Mr Broadchip dropped his last bit of welsh rarebit.

"That old, grizzled gabblesnoot? Well, thank you kindly, but I'm much better-looking than that average-sized lumpling."

"I meant more personality-wise," Nils said.

"But back to *The Book of All Tomorrow's Dreams*," William said firmly.

"It's all very well talking about that book," Anna said, "but I'm more worried about Gribblebob's book, which is all over my brother's hand."

"Actually," said William, "that is something we should talk about. It might have a bearing on things." He looked over at Gribblebob. "Tell us about your book."

Gribblebob drained his blackcurrant cordial and burped the loudest and most disgusting burp he had in his wide selection of deeply unpleasant noises. Mr Broadchip dropped his empty plate with a clatter on the table and turned his hearing aid off.

CHAPTER 24

"**M**y book," started the goblin, "is a very important book. It is called *Gribblebob's Book of Unpleasant Goblins and Other Unnecessary Shadowfolk*. It's a book I worked on for a very long time when I was living on my side of the veil. It took me mumps and mumps and mumps and mumps and mumps to finish and it's very useful indeed."

"So, is it basically just a list of goblins that aren't so nice, then?" asked Nils. Gribblebob gave him a dismissive look.

"You could put it that way," he shifted on his chair slightly, "if you were pignorant."

"Ignorant," corrected Anna, and Gribblebob nodded.

"Yes, yes, you too. Me knows, me knows."

Nils looked over at the goblin. "Why've you started talking all funny like that?" he asked.

"Funny?" repeated Gribblebob, raising a bushy eyebrow. "T'ain't funny at all. It's only that now these two big shamoozles are here and you know all about me, I don't need to put on flares and braces no more, do I? Don't need to blend in with you fussy thumbjabbers. I can let me be me. Let it all hang out. It's a messy belief, to sell the truth."

"Tell us about the book," snapped Jack impatiently.

Gribblebob gave him a withering stare before carrying on. "Before I got tired of all the magic and malarkey over there, I was quite a well-known goblin. My name was spoken in the highest squircles."

"Bobblehead," whispered Anna to Nils really, really softly and Nils giggled slightly, despite still feeling scared about the rip-riders.

"Whassat?" asked Gribblebob, but he ignored them and carried on. "So I was asked by the Great Goblin to put together a book of all the low, thieving, cheating, lying, spickling, downright plain nasty goblins in the world, to sort of keep a track of them all. And as I started, my task grew, and the

Great Goblin also wanted me to list all the other dark, vicious, spippling shadowfolk—the ones not to be trusted, like Folkward Cagewell, the Shixster, that tribe of pixies that live down by the Glazey River, the Tylunas Twins—"

William dipped his head and stifled a little laugh at this point, just to himself, and Gribblebob looked over at him very seriously.

"And of course you're in it, William Wynn."

William looked up and caught the little man's stare. "You know, I thought I might be."

There were a few seconds of uncomfortable silence before Gribblebob continued.

"So's, anyways, I'd done this book, and the Great Goblin puts a spell on it, like a warning spell, so that if you're in the book then us goblins can all recognize you if we happen to meet you on a dark night or a windy market day or whatever, and be on our guard. There's some goblins who don't take kindly to being in the book and would like to have the book and cross out their name or get rids of the book or whatever. Now, the book was kept back on the side of the veil where I comes from orange-a-nelly, but the Great Goblin called me—"

"How?" asked Nils.

"You'se is a questioning boy and no mis-shake," said Gribblebob.

"Yes, but how did he contact you from the other side of the veil?" asked Nils, not giving up.

Gribblebob was quiet for a beat, then said, "Harrier pigeon."

"But—" started Nils.

The little man ignored him and carried on his tale.

"The Great Goblin called me and said he had reasons to believe that the book was in danger, that all magic books were in danger, and he wanted me to break the veil, come and fetch the book and bring it back with me to my home here, to protect it. When you bumped into me today, that's what I was doing. I'd got the book and I was in a hurry to be finding somewhere safe for it."

"So why did it end up all over his hand?" asked Anna.

"Books of magic are more than books. With the spells and whatnots, it's almost like sometimes they can thinks for their shelves. And, thinking about it now, and hearing about the other book, the _really important_ book," he looked over at Jack and William with contempt, "it seems to me that my book was scared. It wanted to hides itself somewhere safe. Magic books have a knickknack of finding people of good, honest heart and kind thoughts. And, much as it spains me to say so, I reckon my book felt that in you and used its magic to hop on over out of the—what would you call it?—out of the sleeve of the book itself, out of the material and actually into you, to hide in you until the danger's passed."

He stopped and looked over at Nils, and at his hand.

"So's I was wrong to says you stole it. I'm slurry."

"Do you mean 'sorry'?" asked Anna.

"I saids what I saids," replied the little man, and folded his arms.

Nils was looking deep in thought. "A good, honest heart?" he said, and then he grinned broadly. "Anna," he carried on, "I've kind thoughts and a good heart!" He looked very proud. "Fancy that."

Anna shook her head slightly and smiled too. "Don't get too carried away, little brother. You've also got a Kindle for a hand. You're like a living e-reader."

"But still," he said, "kind thoughts, good heart."

"Oh, put a stock cube in it," blurted Gribblebob. "I wish I'd kept quiet now."

"You know," said William, more to Jack than anyone else, "this could be a real boon. There aren't many people who magic books take a fancy to. Maybe he could be a help with finding *The Book of All Tomorrow's Dreams*?"

"Hmm," was all Jack said.

CHAPTER 25

Standing outside The Tartan Teapot, Gribblebob knelt down and nuzzled the not-there ears of his halfway-there dog, cooing and ahhing a little as he did so. He held out his hand and opened it to reveal half a ginger snap, which Dimple happily snaffled down. It was very peculiar, seeing the biscuit disappear into the nothingness that was Dimple's mouth. As the chomping went on, his neck and upper back began to quiver into view.

The five oddly assorted companions did look a little out of place on the Uppington Down high street. It was slightly past six o'clock and people were making their way home, but it was surprising how many of the passers-by just took into their stride the sight of an impossibly good-looking man with long hair and a bright scarlet frock coat, a tall, muscular man with a sword by his side, a little person dressed like an explosion in a lost-property room, and two children. Maybe people thought the circus was coming to town, or that they were buskers or part of an advertising gimmick, although it wasn't the usual sort of thing Mr McCurdey did to promote The Tartan Teapot. Normally, he went for something bizarre like "Buy one sandwich, get one sandwich half price next Thursday" or "Bread pudding with a pot of bottomless custard", which Mr McCurdey would spend AGES writing in chalk on the blackboard outside his shop, his glasses pushed back on his head and the tip of his tongue poking out of his mouth as he concentrated on swirly Gs and curly Bs. Swords and rock stars were a definite improvement.

Anna stood there glaring at William and Jack, feeling really quite annoyed. Nils was cupping his magicked hand with his right hand, thinking about his good heart and wondering about rip-riders.

"What are we going to do now, then?" she snapped. "You don't want us to break the veil. You don't want to sort out my brother's hand. All you want is to use Nils to help solve your problem. That doesn't seem at all fair."

"I don't mind, sis," said Nils happily. "Us kind and good ones like to help as much as we can."

Anna sighed. Her brother was going to be insufferable from now on.

"Our problem," replied Jack sternly, "is actually everyone's problem. Mara could bring her nightmare plague to both sides of the veil. And if the book is this side, then so is she, most likely."

"And once we've tracked down that book, we can help sort out your brother's hand." William reached out and placed his hand on Anna's shoulder. "I promise."

Despite herself, Anna shivered. It was strange with William. He looked nice and kind, and she found herself drawn to like him, but when his hand was on her shoulder she felt something else, just beneath the surface—something a little darker than she would have liked.

"You're in the book though," she said, "of, what was it, liars—"

"Thieving, cheating, lying, spickling, vicious, spippling downright nasty characters," said Gribblebob.

"A misunderstanding." William smiled. "I am not always appreciated for my very singular talents."

Gribblebob snorted.

"William," said Jack, and William Wynn turned to his compatriot. "You said you had an idea of where the book might be, who might have it."

"Is that what I said?" William shrugged and ran his hand through his hair. "Perhaps I might have been a little optimistic there."

Jack sighed deeply. "You never change, do you, William?"

"But I do know where we can start. Someone did mention a name to me."

"And?..."

"Omeria Toureau."

"Ms Toureau!" echoed the children.

"But she's our school librarian," explained Anna. "How on earth can she know anything?"

At the mention of the word "school", Jack seemed to blanch slightly, and he had a most disconcerting feeling, as if he was slipping out of himself, as if he was falling down and deep, as if he was passing somebody on the way, somebody he knew and yet had never met.

"Jack?" asked William, looking concerned, but Jack just shook his head and gathered himself. He was a warrior of the True Dreamers, after all.

"Your little friend there isn't the only one who prefers living on this side of the veil," he said to

Anna. "I think you'd be surprised at quite how many folk there are who have broken the rules."

"Is Mr McCurdey one?" asked Nils.

"No," said Jack, puzzled. "Why do you ask?"

"No reason," said Nils, sneaking a glance at Gribblebob.

"So we go to the school, then," stated William.

"It's shut now," volunteered Nils.

"But Ms Toureau will still be there, I bet," said Anna. "She's always beavering away at something in the library."

"Fine. Lead the way, young lady, lead the way." William bowed very slightly at the waist.

"Ms Toureau told us she came from Trinidad though," said Nils.

"I could tell you I come from Cleethorpes. That don't make me a cabbage, do it?" said Gribblebob.

"Do you know," said Nils, "half the time I have no idea what you're talking about."

"Covfefe," said Gribblebob, nodding.

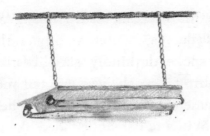

CHAPTER 26

It was a pleasant autumn night, and the sun was starting to set as they headed to the school. Most lights were out, but they could see that the library lights, on the ground floor, were shining. The group walked around to the big windows, and Anna knocked on the glass. From behind a bookshelf, Ms Toureau's head popped out and she made her way to the window. When she recognized Anna, she smiled and nodded with her head to the entrance door nearest the library. They waited outside, and eventually they heard the clatter of locks and the door opened.

Ms Toureau appeared.

"Why, Anna Bryton, hello, sweet. Bit late to be borrowing a book, isn't it?" she said, smiling.

"Hello, Ms Toureau," said Anna. "We're sorry to bother you..."

As she spoke, the kindly faced librarian took in Nils, the little man, the wagging tail and the two tall gentlemen bringing up the rear. When she saw Jack and William, her smile faded like wallpaper in the sun.

"Oh," she said, "you'd all better come in," and she stepped back and opened the door wide for them to enter.

As Jack entered the school, he started to feel queasy. He didn't know why, and he kept it to himself, but something didn't feel right. He didn't like being here. It didn't feel safe. It felt like the world of wide-open terror. He rested his hand on the hilt of his sword again, for comfort.

Ms Toureau led the way to the warm, welcoming lights of the library. "I must say, I'm quite surprised to see the company you're keeping tonight," she said to the children over her shoulder. "Aren't you going to introduce me?"

"This is William Wynn," said Nils, nodding his head towards William.

"And this is 'Jack Broadsword'," said Anna, saying the name as if it were in quotation marks.

Jack gave her a funny look as she did so. He felt

that stretching again, that waking-up sensation, from somewhere hidden, and the name growing within him came breathing into his ear again, louder this time. *Bengt.*

"Pleasure," said William, bowing slightly.

"Greetings to you," said Jack, and dipped his head.

"Yes, I've heard of both of you. My name is Omeria Toureau," replied the librarian, and she held out her hand to shake theirs, one ring of bright silver with a small blue stone glittering against her dark skin.

"And I'm the rat's brother," said Gribblebob.

"Oh, sorry, I forgot you," apologized Anna.

"Ah, Mr Robert Gribble," Ms Toureau said, with a slightly amused expression on her face, "I believe I've seen you around town."

"Never not noticed you afore," he sniffed.

"I'm discreet," she said, and waved her hand towards Jack and William. "Which is more than I can say for you two."

"Are you really from the other side of the veil?" asked Nils, before either William or Jack could reply.

"Well, now. How extraordinary to be asked such a question, right here in my library. So you know about all of that, do you?" The children nodded. "Then I suppose I have to admit to you that, yes, I do come from the other side of the veil."

"And not from Trinidad, after all?" said Nils, just to clarify. Ms Toureau shrugged slightly and held her hands out, both palms up.

"No, sweet, not from Trinidad after all—well, not the Trinidad you mean." She looked away from the children and up to Jack and William. "I suppose this is about books?" she said, and then carried on before anyone could answer her. "Yes, I've been noticing a few strange things the last few days—in my private collection."

"What sort of things?" asked William.

"Books fading out. Books trying to hide themselves. Books going missing."

"Magic books!" exclaimed Anna. "Have you got magic books in the library?"

"Not exactly," said Ms Toureau. "Not on the shelves to borrow, anyway, but I brought a few select titles with me, good friends. In my office." She nodded over her shoulder to the little room at the back of the library. "When I noticed what was happening with my books, I had a feeling there must be some kind of disturbance affecting all magic books. And with you being here like this, I would hazard a guess that I was not entirely incorrect?"

"No, you're not wrong," nodded William. "I heard a whisper, from someone who knows, that you might have been contacted recently by a person who might have needed some advice from someone like you."

"Someone like you?" repeated Nils. "Are you magic or something, Ms Toureau?"

She smiled at Nils. "I'm a book-keeper," she said.

"Like an accountant?" asked Anna.

Ms Toureau shook her head. "No, not like an accountant. I'm more like a... bee-keeper kind of book-keeper. I look after magical and enchanted books, and keep them buzzing and keep them safe."

"So did someone contact you?" William repeated his question. She looked at him and held his gaze.

"No. Nobody has contacted me."

"Nobody at all? Nobody from our side of the veil?"

She continued holding his gaze, unwavering. "That's what I said."

"Well," said William, running his hand through his hair. "There's a thing."

Jack had been very quiet since they entered the school, and now he could feel a prickling at the back of his neck, and a flip-flopping in his stomach. He felt more scared now than when the tanglewolf had been facing him in the Darkwood. He felt that he was going to start shaking.

And he had no idea why.

CHAPTER 27

"The thing is," said William, "the person who gave me your name is not normally the sort of person who gets things wrong. And that person was very certain indeed you had been contacted by someone about a certain book."

Ms Toureau leant back against the library counter—where only the other day Anna had checked out *Don't Let Your Yesterdays Waste Your Tomorrows*, a really good poetry book—and crossed her legs at the ankles. "Even that kind of a person can make mistakes," she said, crossing her arms, "I suppose."

It went very quiet, and Anna felt as if the temperature in the library had dropped by a few degrees. She looked over at Jack, who was shivering, and guessed he must feel it too. But was it really that cold?

William looked over at the goblin. "Gribblebob, my gallant, unkempt friend, we know I am in your book of untrustworthy creatures and so forth. Tell me, would our fine, friendly book-keeper here also happen to be in that book of yours?"

The goblin looked from William to Ms Toureau, and back to William.

"Can't nightly say. Don't recall the name, and since me book went hibbledy-squibbledy into young fellow-my-lad over there, I've not been getting any warnings. Didn't even get a warning when I saw you. Remembered your name, is all."

Ms Toureau uncrossed her arms, laid them behind her, resting her palms on the desk, and in a hurt voice said, "Why, Mr Wynn. Anyone would think you were casting aspersions on my hard-won reputation. I am a school librarian, you know."

"And a good one," said Anna, who was a little surprised at how the atmosphere in the room had changed.

"Well, thank you, sweet," said Ms Toureau warmly. "It's always nice to be appreciated." Then she looked back at William and continued, "And what is the book I was supposed to have been asked about?"

William said nothing, and Nils began to fill in the awkward silence.

"It's called *The Book of*—"

"It's of no matter," William said sharply, interrupting him, "if my sources were wrong this time."

Nils looked to the floor and Ms Toureau smiled sweetly at William. "Everyone gets things wrong sometimes, Mr Wynn. Even you."

The room went quiet again, and Anna didn't like how it felt. "What books do you have, Ms Toureau?" she asked. "I can't believe there were magic books here in the school all the time and I never knew."

"Books of spells, books of protection, a few others..." The librarian's voice trailed off and she pushed herself away from the desk and addressed William again. "I have to say, Mr Wynn, I do wonder about the wisdom of letting two children from here"—she waved a hand in the air—"know all about our side of the veil, about magic books and..." Again, her voice trailed off. "No disrespect to you two, of course," she said to Anna and Nils.

"It was me toldum," said Gribblebob. "Didn't have no choice, with young fella-me-lad having me book all over his hand."

"Oh," said Ms Toureau, suddenly sharply inter-
ested. "Show me?"

Before William or anyone else could say anything, Nils held his arm and hand out and spread
his fingers wide so the characters could be seen
scrolling at speed across his skin.

"My word," exclaimed the librarian. "What an
extraordinary boy you must be." She reached out to
take Nils's hand in hers, but to his own surprise he
jerked his hand back before she could. He'd simply
had a deep feeling inside that he shouldn't let her
touch his hand, or rather, that what was in his hand
wouldn't allow her to touch it. "Extraordinary,"
she repeated, slightly more steel-edged this time.

"Good heart and kind of thought," said Jack,
and everybody looked at him in surprise as it had
been such a long time since he had said anything.

"Just so, Mr Broadsword," said Ms Toureau,
looking back at Nils. "Just so."

CHAPTER 28

"**W**e should leave," said William, looking hard at Ms Toureau. "Sorry to have wasted your time."

"Always nice to see someone else from... Trinidad," she replied, with a little grin. "But surely you won't be taking the children with you? I don't think they really belong with you, do they? This is their school, after all, and besides," she turned to the children before William could say anything, "wouldn't you two like to see my special books? Now that you know about the veil, perhaps it wouldn't hurt."

"Oh, please," said Anna instinctively, but Nils still felt something inside from when the librarian had tried to take his hand.

"School's shut," he said, "and I want to stay

with William, Jack and him." He nodded his head towards the goblin.

"Yes, we're leaving," said William decisively.

"Mmm." Ms Toureau frowned and drew her lips into a thin, straight line as she shook her head from side to side. "You know, I really don't think *they* are." Just as she finished speaking, all the blinds in the library windows suddenly crashed down and the door to her office slammed shut. The children and the goblin jumped, Jack started shivering more and William took a step towards the librarian.

Ms Toureau held up a hand, palm outwards, facing William.

"Don't come any closer, Mr Wynn. You and your shivery friend and Mr Robert Gribble there are free to go. In fact, I insist on it." And as she said that, the main door to the library flew open with a wisp of wind. "But the children stay with me."

"What are you?" asked William. "When I was told about you, I was told you were a book-keeper, a good, knowledgeable book-keeper, but not that you had magic in you like this."

Ms Toureau ignored William's question and held up her other hand, palm upwards, towards him.

"Leave," was all she said, and then it was as if there was a tunnel of wild wind blasting towards William and forcing him back towards the open library door. As he slid back across the waxed wooden floor, his hands reached out and grabbed at the bookshelves as he passed them, sending books tumbling to the floor in a flutter of pages.

"What's happening?" shrieked Nils, in real terror. Anna rushed over to her little brother and put her arm around him, pulling him close and feeling his whole body vibrate with fear.

"Leave!" repeated Ms Toureau, more loudly this time, and her voice had a slightly different tone now, as if it were made up of a thousand soft screams, all held together by an anger and a fear that was on the edge of coming apart at any second. "LEAVE!"

William went slipping back towards the open door, his trailing hands leaving a clatter of books in his wake. He tried to say something, tried to do something, tried to do the same thing he had done when he had helped Jack with the tanglewolf in the Darkwood, but the pressure of the wind on his chest drew the breath from his lungs and the spit from his mouth. His eyes teared up, and he was helpless. As William neared the door, he looked over at Jack, who was leaning against a far wall of books, shivering.

Dimple started barking wildly, but Gribblebob didn't even bother to try and silence his halfway-there dog as he watched the librarian, or whatever she was, send tall William Wynn out of the library with a final, fearsome flourish. The door slammed shut after him.

"What—" began Anna.

"Quiet!" said Ms Toureau firmly. Then, softer, "sweet." She turned to Gribblebob. "You and your yapping hound can take the window." She held up one hand, and as she did so, the goblin and his dog were lifted up off the floor of the library in a powerful flurry of gusts and went flying towards one of the big library windows.

"Gerroffameeee!" shouted out Gribblebob, and barely a heartbeat before he and Dimple went smashing through the glass, the window opened to let them out, squeaking shut again a moment later.

While this was going on, Jack had drawn his broadsword, although with trouble, as his hands were shaking so much and he felt weak and breathless. He moved towards Omeria Toureau, while her eyes were watching the goblin and his pet fly out of the window. Once the window flew shut, she turned to the advancing warrior.

"Mr Broadsword. Living up to your name, I see. Now, I wonder where I shall send you. The door? The window? Or maybe I'll crush you here, instead. I don't really like the look of that sword..."

"DON'T!" shouted Anna, and Ms Toureau turned to the girl.

"I've told you once to be quiet, sweet. Don't make me have to tell you twice." As Ms Toureau said this, Anna shrunk back against her brother, holding him tight to her. The librarian turned back to Jack.

"You know, I think I will crush you, after all."

Just then, there was an almighty flash, like lightning or the millions of crystals in a snowstorm suddenly igniting, and in the howl of thundering waves of light, the children were blown off their feet to the floor, Ms Toureau was thrown back across her desk, several bookshelves toppled over and about a half-dozen lightbulbs exploded at the same time. There was a hazy mist where Jack had been standing, and as it dissipated up into the crackled electricity surrounding the exploded lights, it could be seen that Jack was no longer there.

Bengt Arbuthnot was.

CHAPTER 29

William lay on his back on the cold, hard school corridor floor and felt the breath gradually returning to his body. His eyes were shut, his chest and stomach hurt where the force of the wind had pummelled him and the backs of his legs ached from trying to withstand its immense force. His fingers were sore where he had grabbed at the bookshelves. It had been a very long time since William had been unable to use his very particular abilities to protect himself or others around him. But in the library, no matter how much he had willed himself, he hadn't been able to transform into what he needed to be, into that creature that wasn't quite a bat, not exactly a raven, but no longer only a man. Something had been stopping him.

It was like trying to push against a bolted door. It frustrated and angered him. Suddenly there was a huffy panting sound and a wet, raspy tongue was licking at his face.

"I don't think he likes you," said Gribblebob, and William opened his eyes to see the goblin standing over him and the nearly-there dog by his face, licking him enthusiastically. "I just think he's curious about how you taste. So don't let it go to your head."

William pushed the dog away gently and sat up. The bits of Dimple you could see started to get licked by the bits of Dimple you couldn't see.

"Where's Jack?" asked William. The goblin nodded towards the locked library door.

"In there, I 'pose. He hasn't been chucked out, anyhoo."

"And the boy and the girl?"

"Same."

William stood up and dusted off his coat and his trousers. He stretched and cursed softly at the various aches and pains.

"I was prized you didn't do that thing you normally do," said the goblin. "I was almost looking forward to seeing it up close, like."

"I was rather surprised myself."

"It's a paw full of quiet in there," said the goblin, reaching over to Dimple. "Oh, don't do that, boy," he said, "'t ain't savoury." The dog stopped its licking spree and smacked its chops instead. "Are we going to go back in, then?"

"If we can," said William. He drew himself up to his full height, put his head back, blew out a breath of air between pursed lips and shook his head so his long hair flew out and round. There was a beating of wings and a flurry of darkness as, this time, he was able to will himself to change, to transform into his other self or, maybe, just perhaps, his true self.

CHAPTER 30

Bengt looked around the library in huge surprise. The last thing he remembered—well, the last thing he properly remembered—was being sat under his favourite tree with his notepad, his good pen and his favourite pastime of being people other than him. He did have some sort of half-memory of being called, of being yanked out of himself, and rising then tumbling and falling, and some wisps of things not quite seen, and of sleeping, and of waking up extremely slowly, like on a summer Sunday morning with the brightness shining through the gap where the curtains don't quite meet and lighting up the dust motes spiralling lazily overhead. But those half-memories did not feel as hard and as sharp as the wooden floor under his feet and the fallen down bookshelves, scattered books and bits of broken lightbulb he could see everywhere.

There was a soft moaning from the big library desk, and as he stretched his neck to see, the librarian, Ms Toureau, was in the process of setting herself up on her knees, one hand on the desk.

"Bengt?" he heard, and looking to the other side of the desk he saw Anna, from his year, and her younger brother. What was his name again? Neil?

"Anna?" he responded. "What's going on?"

"Where's Jack?" asked Nils.

"Jack?" said Bengt, his third question in a row.

"Jack Broadsword," said Anna, and Bengt stiffened. How did they know about one of his secret names? Had they gotten hold of his book? What if they gave it to Mandy? No, Anna wouldn't do that, she wasn't like that. All this was going through his mind as Ms Toureau staggered gingerly to her feet. She put one hand to her face and blinked once or twice, her vision steadying, and then she saw Bengt.

"Oh," she said, "and do we have another extraordinary boy with us today, I wonder?"

"Ms Toureau?" And there was Bengt's fourth question in a row. He was starting to feel more and more stupid about not understanding anything that was going on. But even though he felt slightly stupid, he also felt, in a strange way, he was meant to be here.

The librarian ignored Bengt and turned to the other two children. "However, the extraordinary boy I need just now is the one who has books in his fingertips. I have use of you. Come here." She stretched out her hand towards Nils and wriggled her fingers at him. "Now."

Nils stood stock-still next to his sister and held on to her tighter.

"Before I get tetchy again," said Ms Toureau.

Nils made no sign of moving.

Ms Toureau blew out a breath of frustration, and with one quick movement, in a burst of bright wind, the librarian was suddenly right by Nils. The ring on her finger flashed as she grabbed him by the ear and yanked him roughly from the protective arm of his sister.

"OW!" he shouted.

"Let him go!" screamed Anna at the same time.

There was suddenly a smash of breaking glass and a huge, dark, winged creature flew through a shattering window, heading towards the librarian with a screech and squeal of anger, sharp silver claws and hungry, shining teeth eager for her.

Ms Toureau put up her hands, palms out, as if to conjure the same furious winds as before, but this time the airborne animal, seemingly made of mist and shadow and sharp edges, was too fast and too wild and too angry, and it reached her before the wind could start. It dived straight for her face. Claws sliced, teeth bit and the librarian screamed.

She put her hands to her face and tried to pull the frenzied shadowbeast off, but the creature had too much of a hold, and its teeth and claws were in too deep. Her scream grew, but now it came from deeper inside her, and a thick, sticky oil of evil started to run from the cuts and the bites, where you might have expected blood to flow, and Ms Toureau's body went limp as the oil ran faster and faster out of her, and swirled into a black, twisting, streaming figure, eyes wide with fear and loathing, mouth stretched with shrieks, before it misted away into a soft implosion of nothingness and only the echo of screams.

The dark, winged creature loosed itself from the librarian's face, and in a flutter of wings and claws and teeth was gone. Only William Wynn was left standing there, and he knelt quickly down and cradled the body of Ms Toureau, who was now bleeding red, not black.

"Rip-rider," he said.

"I-I..." stammered Anna, and Nils turned his face away. Bengt stood staring right at William Wynn. He knew him in some way, recognized him. But from where?

There was tinkle of glass by the window and Gribblebob climbed in. He took just one look at Ms Toureau in William's arms and turned to Nils.

"There's not many minutes left inside her. She'll need a-fixing." He nodded towards the back office, with its closed door. "In there, she said she had books of protection. Fetch one."

"ME?" shouted Nils, tears starting in his eyes. "I don't know! I wouldn't know."

"You don't needs to know. The way my book went and slurped its way on you, it seems books of magic take a liking to you."

"Remember, you've got a good and kind heart," said Anna, and squeezed her brother's hand.

"You'll be picking the one which works," said the goblin, and nodded his head. Nils waited a second, Anna nudged him, and then he went running to the office.

"That... that horrible thing," was all Anna could say.

"Yep. Pretty dizzy gusting, weren't it? That's our William Wynn's other face."

"No," said Anna, shaking her head at Gribblebob. "Not that—not him—that other thing, the screaming thing."

"Ah," said the goblin, "*that* horrible thing."

"It was a rip-rider," William said quietly, still cradling the limp body of Ms Toureau in his arms. "It had taken her, was inside her. Making her do what Mara wanted. I should have guessed. Stupid of me. When I attacked her, when, when my... magic, if you can call it that, my... well, me, when I reached inside her, it panicked and fled, left her. Left her like... like this." Anna could see that some blood was pooling by William's knees where he was holding her.

"Got it!" They turned as Nils came rushing out of the office, a small, slim, slippery book falling from one hand to the other so that it looked like he was juggling with it. "I went in and this book seemed to flip towards me." He reached William and handed him the book, but William didn't take it.

"Hold it over her heart and open it," he instructed Nils.

"But—"

William just looked up at Nils, and Nils did as he was told. He moved closer to the librarian, and held the book out over her chest, near where he thought her heart was.

"More to the middle," said Anna, remembering her biology lessons.

"I know," muttered Nils, and opened the book randomly, holding it open over the centre of her chest. As he did so, there was a rattling sound, like windchimes on a rainy day, and a sudden rush of breath from... somewhere, and then a wavering cascade of molten light seemed to pour from the pages of the book down into Ms Toureau. Her body shook, she took a huge gulp of air, and the blood pooling by William seemed to shrink back and vanish into the librarian. The ragged holes where tooth and claw had done their damage knitted together and after a second or three, her eyes fluttered open.

"Ow," she said quietly.

"Don't see that every day," said the goblin. "Leastways, not in Uppington Down. And on a Wednesday too."

CHAPTER 31

William continued cradling the wounded librarian, who was now leaning up against his shoulder. Her cuts had healed to thin, pale scratches, but she seemed to be very weak.

"I'm sorry," said William softly. "I had no choice. There was nothing else to be done."

Ms Toureau looked up into his eyes. "Did you know?... Did you know it was in me?"

"I..." William could not finish his sentence, and as his voice trailed off Bengt moved towards them. He had picked up Ms Toureau's cardigan, which had been blown from the back of her chair, and now he laid it gently over her chest to help keep her warm. He'd seen on TV news stories that people in shock were often given blankets.

"There," he said, and as he spoke, his eyes locked with William's, and he felt it again: a connection, a sensation that he somehow knew this strange man. William nodded and turned back to Ms Toureau, who continued talking.

"It was making me say things, do things. Not forcing me, but more like guiding me, suggesting what to say, making me feel I needed to do what it wanted. It felt right. I couldn't stop it. Any of it."

William nodded. "That's what they do. Once they're in you, they make you feel that what you are doing is the right thing to do."

"But all the time I was doing what it suggested, there was a part of me that was somewhere else, in a nightmare somewhere, falling, flying, screaming, taking me far from home... There were faces at windows, calling to me, faces that... Oh, I don't even want to remember." She became very still and quiet.

Bengt felt funny inside while she was talking about a part of her being somewhere else, about falling and flying. He knew those feelings.

"I need to ask you..." said William. "Someone came and spoke to you about *The Book of All Tomorrow's Dreams*, didn't they?"

The librarian shifted her position and grimaced at a shot of pain. "Yesterday. I was working late in the library; my books had been restless, so I knew something was going on. I was half expecting something, but not what actually happened." She sighed deeply and closed her eyes.

"Please," said William. "What happened?"

She opened her eyes again and looked directly into his. "So you really didn't know I had that thing in me? You weren't just trying to get it out of me?"

"Please," William repeated, avoiding her question and what it meant—that he wasn't trying to rescue her, but to stop her. Any way he could.

She paused and looked away from him. "Hobley Brown came. I glanced up from my desk and there he was, silent and smiling. With a package under his arm."

"Hobley Brown? That old retro crate," said Gribblebob. "I thought his toes had curled many a moon ago."

"Go on," urged William.

"I asked him what he was doing this side of the veil. I told him I wanted nothing to do with whatever sour-faced plan he was hatching."

"Hoo-hoo, bet he liked that," sniggered the goblin. Ms Toureau ignored him and continued.

"He told me he'd come into rather a treasure, and he needed my help. He took the package from under his arm, tore open the wax paper wrapping and I saw what he had. He told me he couldn't open the book, that the binding spell was too strong, that he needed a book-keeper's help. I told him I would never help him, and then, the next thing I know, a rip-rider appeared from behind him and... and... and then it was inside me and I had no choice, there was nothing I could do.

"I helped him to open the book. I wanted to help him open it. It felt so good when I managed to find the right pattern, the easy sequence, the golden turn, and the heavy front cover opened for the first time in hundreds of years. Oh, I'm so sorry!" She started to cry.

"Bit late for all that malarkey now," said Gribblebob.

"Hush," William whispered, to both Ms Toureau and the goblin. "Hush, now."

"But where's the book now, then?" asked Anna, who'd been listening intently.

"Hobley Brown said he had to take it to Mara, but there was one more thing to be done before the spell could be truly broken and the Rider could feast on dreams and let the nightmares flow again. The book, as it is now? It's like an unexploded firework."

"A firework? A book like an unexploded firework,"

exclaimed Gribblebob. "I think you gone and dug your claws in a little too deep, William Wynn. She's done gone doolapittydappity."

"You do go on, you know," Nils said crossly.

"It's a hobby," said the little man, shrugging.

"What I've done," carried on Ms Toureau, "is to prepare it. Like when you have a firework, or a rocket, and first you have to remove the safety cap and prepare the fuse—that's what I've done. I've got the firework ready, but now it needs the flame set to the fuse, so the rocket can explode..."

"And so, where's the flame?" asked William. "What does Hobley Brown need to break the spell properly and open the book fully?"

"He needs to wash the book in the tears of a pure-hearted warrior," she explained. "But those tears must have been shed in honest sorrow and found on this side of the veil, or else the spell won't be broken everywhere."

"The tears of a pure-hearted warrior, shed in sorrow. Here?" murmured William.

"Ten-a-penny, them," said Gribblebob.

But those words, *pure-hearted warrior*, had stirred something within Bengt. It felt as if something else—or maybe somebody else—was coming to life inside him.

CHAPTER 32

Elsewhere, under a familiar tree in the Darkwood, another pure-hearted warrior lay, spat-out and exhausted.

Jack Broadsword propped himself up on one elbow, his head spinning and woozy. He had a feeling of having been pulled out of himself, of being sent back, of having done enough. It was such a strange sensation—of being pulled and thrown and tumbled and torn through the veil in the places where it was weakest. He also felt that he'd left... what? Something of himself behind. No, wait, that wasn't quite right—he hadn't lost anything, it was more like he'd shared something of himself, that he'd opened his heart and someone had dipped their hands in and touched the essence of who he was.

He couldn't keep his eyes open any longer, a heavy tiredness spread slowly over him, like honey off a spoon, and he fell back on the soft grass into a long and gentle sleep.

CHAPTER 33

Bengt had no real idea what was going on, what the time was or what was up with the very tall stranger and the equally short stranger—and could he smell a dog in here? People were using his secret, made-up names, he had somehow got from his tree to the library—which was in a state guaranteed to give Mr Cobbister the caretaker a red-faced fit—without knowing how, there were bat-like bird-foxes crashing in through the window and changing into fashion-model-men who he seemed to know from somewhere, he had the oddest sensation that somehow he knew exactly what a pure-hearted warrior was, and, most annoying of all, he seemed to have lost his best pen.

He was starting to get rather ticked off.

"Can I just ask," he piped up, when the conversation had stopped for a moment, "what the flip is going on?"

"Language," murmured Gribblebob, but everyone ignored him.

William had noticed the boy earlier, and he had seen something in his eyes when he had laid the cardigan over the librarian, but with everything that had been going on, this was the first time he really looked at him. And when he looked at him, the first thought that came into William's mind was Jack. He glanced around the library looking for Jack, but he couldn't see him, only his abandoned broadsword resting on the floor by the far wall.

"Where's Jack?" he asked.

"There was, like, an explosion or something," answered Anna. "Then he was just... gone."

"And Bengt was here instead," went on Nils.

"You're Bengt?" William asked the other boy, who nodded. William took another long, deep look at him, so that Bengt started to feel a little uncomfortable. "And are you too one of the True Dreamers?" he finally asked.

Bengt felt flustered at having been so deeply looked at. He didn't think anyone had ever really seen him in quite the way William had just then. And why did he feel that he had heard the phrase "True Dreamers" before?

"I-I haven't a clue what you're on about," he stuttered, looking at William.

"No," said William, standing up carefully and at the same time helping Ms Toureau over to a chair. "I can see that, but I think you need to pick up that sword lying on the floor over there and bring it with us."

Bengt looked over to where the huge, grey, silver-handled sword was resting on the dark wood floor.

"That? I'll never be able to lift that," he spluttered.

"Oh, I think you'll find you can. Try. You'll surprise yourself."

"Bring it with us?" Anna repeated. "Where is it we're going?" As she spoke to William, her eyes followed Bengt, who was hesitantly walking over to the broadsword.

"I think we should go and visit the Grey Lady," he replied, easing the librarian into the chair and making her comfortable. "Will you be okay for a while on your own?" he asked her, and she nodded.

Bengt had knelt down and taken hold of the sword hilt with both hands. He expected it to be much too heavy to lift, but to his amazement it felt no heavier than a cricket bat or hockey stick—well, maybe a little heavier, but it didn't feel impossible or wrong. It actually felt quite right.

"Not the Grey Lady," said Gribblebob, looking over at Bengt, who was now standing straight, holding the sword upright with both hands and admiring it. "She's absolutely twoboggleswoggle crazy. She's got more hats in her bell tree than I've had soft dinners."

"Is she from your side of the veil too?" asked Nils.

"Yep. She's one of our lot," answered the goblin, nodding.

"You know," said Nils, "considering that you say it's forbidden to break the veil, quite a lot of people seem to have come from your side to our side. It seems to me that the Court of Naughtiness isn't doing a very good job."

"Wills and ways," said the goblin, "wills and ways."

"How is it the other way round?" Nils asked. "Are there many of us living there?"

"Not so's you'd note it. I know of maybe two. And one of them simply got lost on the way to the dumplegrounds with his pre-titled cardboard, so really only one who chose to."

"Got lost?" said Nils. "Can't they find their way back?"

"The dumplegrounds is a big place. Not so squeezy to find your way back from there."

"When you say 'pre-titled cardboard' and the 'dumplegrounds', do you mean the municipal tip and recycling centre on Halfberry Road?" clarified Nils.

"I means the dumplegrounds," said the goblin, "on Fullberry Avenue."

"I think it would be very interesting to visit your side of the veil one day," said Nils.

"Not the dumplegrounds," sniffed Gribblebob. "Not very interesting at all. Besides, stinks like the back of an old man's ear."

Anna had walked over to Bengt, who was turning the sword around in his hands to take in the different angles. "You don't seem to have too much trouble lifting it after all," she said.

"It's weird, you know," he replied. "It's not at all as heavy as I thought. It actually feels really good, even if..."

"Even if it's almost as big as you," finished Anna.

"Weird," he repeated.

William, who had been making sure Ms Toureau would be okay on her own, now clapped his hands loudly so that everyone jumped, stopped talking and turned to him.

"Now, my friends," he said, "we have a place to go and a person to see."

"Yeah, a twoboggleswoggle crazy person," muttered the goblin under his breath, and Dimple barked.

CHAPTER 34

It seemed that the Grey Lady lived out at the back of Henchurch Farmhouse, which wasn't actually a farmhouse any more, but was now a community centre. They had salsa dancing there on a Saturday, bingo on a Tuesday. There was a small brick bungalow standing on its own at the end of a higgledy-piggledy lane behind Henchurch Farmhouse, which Anna, Bengt and Nils had never noticed before. Gribblebob knew exactly where to go, so he and Dimple led the way. All the Uppington Down streetlights had come on now, but there weren't any along the lane, so it was fairly dark.

As they walked, Bengt and the other two children talked.

"What's going on though, Anna? This is all just mad, isn't it?"

"You're the one carrying a sword along Uppington Down high street." Anna smiled.

"Okay, yes, but what's up with Neil's hand?"

"Nils," said Nils. "'Kay? Nils, not Neil."

"Kill a snot eel?" said Gribblebob. "Yuck! Sounds dizzy gusting."

"Sorry," said Bengt, ignoring the goblin, which generally appeared to be the most sensible thing to do. "Nils. But?..."

"I got a magic book caught in my hand. But it's because I've got a good heart and kind thoughts, so that's all good."

"Ohhhkay," said Bengt, giving Nils a look before continuing. "Earlier, everyone was talking about a Jack. Jack"—and here he paused briefly, as it felt a bit odd to be using this name with other people— "Broadsword. What—I mean, who... who's he?"

"He's William's friend," Anna explained, "from the other side of the veil."

"Yes, people keep talking about that too. But what does it mean?"

"Long story short," said the goblin, who'd been listening again, "so's it's squeezy to thunderstand. World of magic. Exists here, exists there. There's a...

well, think of it as a magic curtain that cuts that world, world of magic, from this world, world of motoring cars and selling phones. Called *the veil*. Worlds are connected in lots of odd ways. Here, Uppington Down, there, Downington Upp. Here, Robert Gribble, there, Gribblebob. Clear?"

"Um."

"Good. I likes a quick learner. Hurry up, Dimple!" he called, and he chivvied up his almost-there dog.

"I also have questions about that dog with bits missing," said Bengt, "but I think they can wait."

"Probably for the best," agreed Anna wisely. She knew Bengt a little: they were in the same year, but not the same form group. He had always seemed very shy, and it seemed as though Mandy Musgrave and her band of unmentionables picked on him all the time. Sometimes Anna felt like she wanted to step in and say something, or do something, but then she was a bit afraid that she would be in Mandy's firing line instead. Sometimes Bengt had said clever, funny things that made her smile, but often he kept quiet. Anna thought he had a nice, kind face, but a bit of a sad face.

"But, Jack Broadsword..." he continued.

"Yes?" She smiled. "Sounds like a made-up name, doesn't it?"

"Exactly!" he exclaimed. "It sounds just like a made-up name, just like Oscar Oakheart or Will Summersky or..."

"Bertie Beetroot," said Nils.

"Yes, Bertie—well, no, actually, not like Bertie Beetroot." Bengt shook his head. "But the other names. Oscar, Will, Jack—those are all names I made up. Jack Broadsword *is* a made-up name and I made it up."

"Well, no," said Nils, "because Jack is real and we've both met him, and... you're carrying his sword."

"So where is he now then?" asked Bengt.

"He just disappeared," said Anna. "And you appeared."

"But that's all crazy."

"It's been that sort of a day," said Anna, shrugging.

"And on a Wednesday," said Nils, who'd been listening too much to Gribblebob. "Imagine."

They had slowed down, as they were coming close to the Grey Lady's bungalow.

"All right, my friends," said William. "We're nearly there."

"I've been thinking, though," asked Anna.

"Yes, fair lady?" William full-beamed.

"About the rip-rider, the one you scared out of Ms Toureau..."

"Hmm?" William nodded, his full-beam dimming a little.

"Is it... is it just gone now? Or, or is it floating around somewhere? I mean, what I mean is—"

"Yes," he interrupted her. "I think that is the answer to the question you would rather not ask. Yes, the rip-rider could return and could attempt to ride one of us. But I do feel I weakened it."

"Oh," was all Anna could say.

"Also," said Nils, filling the gap, "are you a vampire?"

"What?" William laughed and drew his hand through his long hair. "A vampire? Me? No."

"But you turn into a bat."

"A bat? No. Not a bat."

"Well, you turn into something."

"Or maybe something turns into him," said Bengt suddenly, and everyone turned to look at him.

William's eyes narrowed slightly.

"Sorry," said Bengt nervously, dropping his gaze to the floor. "I don't really know where that came from."

"But anyway," went on Nils, "you turn into some type of creature, and it has wings and can fly and has sharp teeth and talons and you drink blood."

"Drink blood!" repeated William aghast. Nils merely pointed at William's T-shirt, the one that had a picture of a bat's head and said *Drink Blood* on it.

"But you told me that your Uncle Oscar had one just like it. Does that make your Uncle Oscar a vampire?"

"He does mainly come out at night," said Anna, smiling.

"Vampire," smirked Gribblebob, under his breath.

"I have a question too," said Bengt. "What's a True Dreamer?"

"Ah!" said the goblin. "Now, then. There's a story and a third. But to spit out the nut of it... they're old blood. Not shadowfolk, not magic, but they are closer to the things of nature and one step nearer the veil than normal folk. They feel things on their fingertips, see things out of the corner of their eye that most people miss."

Dimple barked, and the goblin reached into his pocket and fetched out the other half of the ginger snap, which was gratefully gobbled up, causing the dog's head to begin coming into view.

"But why True Dreamers?" pressed Bengt, as Gribblebob ruffled Dimple's neck.

"Good boy... Because they hear things in their dreams, get told things, things that end up coming true."

"So—"

"Enough!" William said firmly. "The Grey Lady's abode lies just ahead."

"You still haven't told us why we need to talk to her," Anna said.

"No, I haven't, have I?" William replied, and he made his way up the higgledy-piggledy path.

CHAPTER 35

William stood at the door of the bungalow, Gribblebob by his side, with Dimple slightly behind, then Anna and Nils, side by side, and Bengt bringing up the rear. William rapped heavily on the door and waited.

No response.

"It's Wednesday," Gribblebob said. "Probably out at bingo or pingball or whatever it is they call it with the trampolines and whatnot." Anna, Nils and Bengt all looked at each other and just shrugged.

William rapped again, harder this time, and they heard a shuffling behind the door and a jangling of latches. The door swung open, and there stood a little, old, grey lady, totally living up to her name. She had long silver-grey hair, pulled back tight, striking diamond-grey eyes, sparkling and alive, wrinkled skin that looked like it had been dusted all over with fine sugar-ash from a fireplace, a dark, dove-grey silk scarf at her neck, with a grey quartz clasp, a thick blue-grey knitted dress on, plus grey tights and a pair of big, bushy Bugs Bunny slippers, which rather spoilt the ensemble.

"Oh my," she exclaimed, and placed a grey hand over her heart. "Visitors. As I live and breathe." Her lively eyes took in the group on her doorstep. "And such visitors they are. You'd best come in—I don't want the neighbours talking."

"With all gratitude." William bowed slightly and entered, the others following.

She led them to her little living room, which was filled with trinkets and candles and more furniture than you would imagine was strictly necessary in such a small bungalow. There seemed to be tables next to tables, chests of drawers on top of chests of drawers and net curtains double-thick at every window. A TV set was blaring loudly in the corner.

"Oh, that's a good show, that is," said the goblin, "I likes that one," and he started to watch it, until the Grey Lady toddled over and switched it off.

"Bloogers," muttered the goblin. "Never mind, I'll watch it on catch-up."

The little old lady settled herself down into what was obviously her favourite chair, and beckoned the others to sit too.

"Please do make yourselves comfortable. I'd offer you tea and jam sandwiches, but, honestly, I really can't be bothered." She smiled a really sweet old-lady smile. "Besides, I have a feeling you have questions for me. Don't you, William Wynn?" She looked over at the tall man sitting on her couch.

"Grey Lady," he began, "I know you have dwelt on this side of the veil for many a year."

"I do so like the television here," she said, nodding, "and the flushing toilets."

"Holy-loo-ya to that, sister," muttered the goblin under his breath.

"And I know that one of your particular pastimes is to keep a track of those of us who traverse the veil, for your own entertainment."

"Everyone needs a little hobby, William Wynn. Something to keep the mind young and lively. One cannot live by television and toilets alone. Or indeed bingo and trampolines. If you don't have something to keep you young, you shrivel up and decay like an old packet of fish fingers left out in the rain." She turned to Gribblebob and looked him up and down with distaste. "You should think about finding *yourself* a hobby, Robert Gribble, before it's too late."

"Muddy cheek!" blurted out the goblin. "I looks after meself. I'm a fine figure of a goblin, I am."

"If you ask me, Mr Robert Gribble, these days I think you're starting to look rather more like a chipped and hollow garden ornament than the fine figure of a goblin you might well once have been." She crossed her legs at the ankle, so that both the Bugs Bunny slippers seemed to be looking, and laughing, at the goblin.

"Hang on a blooming moment!" Gribblebob began. "Is you calling me a muddy garden gnome? A GNOME?" He was actually starting to get a bit angry now.

"If the fishing rod fits, Mr Gribble, if the fishing rod fits..."

The goblin put his hand on the arm of the sofa and started to raise himself up. "Now you just—"

But William put a hand on his shoulder and pulled him back down.

"Please, Grey Lady, I don't think we have much time. Can you tell us who has recently broken the veil?"

"Told you she was twoboggleswoggle crazy," hissed the goblin at nobody in particular. "Gnome indeed."

"Shh," hushed Anna.

"Very well," said the old lady, and shifted slightly in her seat. She rolled up the sleeve of her dress and exposed a very intricate, very beautiful, very large tattoo that seemed to cover the whole of her forearm—from her wrist up as far as they could see. There was something about the tattoo that stirred something in Bengt. It was the pattern. He felt perhaps he had seen that strange, very unusual pattern somewhere else. But he couldn't think where. Then the Grey Lady placed her other hand on her forearm and closed her eyes. She very gently began to rub her hand up and down the tattooed skin of her arm, and, to the surprise of the children, the grey tattoo started to shimmer and sparkle a little. Immediately after that, small, especially bright pinpricks of light started to thrum and vibrate on the pattern.

"It looks a little bit like one of those shopping-mall maps that shows you how to get to the food court," whispered Nils, but Anna shushed him. She was staring intently at the pattern—she recognized it from somewhere too.

Her eyes remained shut, but the Grey Lady started to talk.

"There's all the usual suspects, the ones who've been here for a while." Her eyes flicked open and she stared for a second at the goblin. "The ones who have outstayed their welcome." Her eyes flicked shut and she continued before Gribblebob could say anything. "But recently there's been... there's been you, William Wynn. There's been... there's been Hobley Brown, and he came with a flurry of rip-riders, which isn't so nice, and... yes, that's it." She stopped, and opened her eyes.

"But what about Jack Broadsword?" asked Anna. "We saw him come through, straight after William."

"Jack Broadsword?" repeated the Grey Lady, and closed her eyes again. The tattoo glowed brighter again. "No, no Jack Broadsword crossed over recently." She opened her eyes and sought out Bengt. "I have the sense that Jack Broadsword has been on this side of the veil for a very long time."

William put his hands through his hair and looked at Bengt. "Hmm," he said.

CHAPTER 36

"**W**e need to know where Hobley Brown is right now," said William finally. "Can you tell us, Grey Lady?"

"Of course I can, William Wynn," she replied, and she was just about to close her eyes and rub her arm again when Anna asked a question.

"But what about Mara? The Rider? Can you see if she's broken the veil too?"

"Oh, my dear child," said the Grey Lady. "Mara doesn't need to break the veil like we do. She goes where she wants, she moves where she will. To her, the veil is nothing more than a puff of wind, a misty swirl. She is here, she is there, she is wherever. Like all her kind, both the good and the bad."

"Aha," said Anna. "I see."

"Dis-pressing, ain't it?" sniffled the goblin.

"Hobley Brown," insisted William.

"Oh my, yes, of course." The Grey Lady closed her eyes and touched her tattoo. There was a glimmering and a glittering, and then after a moment, she took her hand away and opened her eyes.

"Hobley Brown, that nasty piece of work, is currently at the village museum—doing something unspeakable with relics, no doubt."

William Wynn stood up sharply. "Thank you, Grey Lady, you have done us a fine service."

"So much easier than making you tea and jam sandwiches, my dear," she said happily, rolling down her sleeve again.

"Come," urged William, "we must go."

As they stood up and headed for the door, Anna turned to the Grey Lady. "I've never seen you around the village. What do they call you here? They can't just call you 'Grey Lady'."

"Well, my dear, here they call me Mrs Naineen Harma, or sometimes 'that strange old Finnish lady', which I've heard them say when they think I'm busy checking my bingo numbers or my rhubarb."

"But you're not Finnish," said Anna, puzzled.

"And your school librarian doesn't come from Trinidad." The Grey Lady winked.

"How did—" began Anna, but the old lady interrupted her as they reached the door.

"Tell your Granny C I said hello, my dear, and that I might see her at salsa on Saturday."

"But—"

"Tell her to go easy on the tartan. I have a feeling it unsettles Mr Broadchip."

"How?..."

Anna felt like she was being pushed—not unkindly, but very forcefully—out of the door by the little old lady, then the door clanged shut against her back.

"Rude old plumpleprune, ain't she?" smirked the goblin.

"I've known worse," said Nils quietly, looking at the goblin.

"Quickly," instructed William. "We must get to the museum. Anna, lead the way."

So they all followed Anna as she hurried off to the Uppington Down Little Museum of Curiosities and Antiquities.

CHAPTER 37

As they walked briskly down the high street, William asked Gribblebob about the museum.

"Tell me, goblin, why might Hobley Brown be at the museum? Are there exhibits there from our side of the veil?"

"It's a posy billy tea. I ain't not never been. Too much good stuff on the tellybox to waste time going to a building full of old stuff."

Anna shook her head sadly. "You know, you probably do fit in better on our side of the veil than yours."

At this, the goblin gave the widest, happiest smile that Anna had ever seen him give.

"Thanks you! That is the nicey-est thing any one of you thumbjabbers has ever said to me."

"It wasn't meant as a compliment," she said.

"Any compliport in a storm," he said, and continued smiling widely.

"Anna," asked William, "what about you? Can you think of anything really unusual or strange in the museum? Something that doesn't look like it belongs?"

Anna bit her lip and tried to think back to the last time she'd visited. It had been with the school, but they'd mainly looked at things to do with the history of the village, so more the antiquities than the curiosities.

"I don't know," she answered. "Not really, but..."

Anna started to think about all the strange things they'd seen today. It really had been a most unusual Wednesday, so far.

"But maybe... maybe the tattoo on the Grey Lady's arm. Maybe I've seen something in the museum with that sort of pattern on. What about you, Bengt? Can you remember seeing anything like it?"

Bengt looked over at Anna. He remembered being at the museum with her and the others from their history class that day. He thought hard about the pattern on the old lady's arm—the way the swirls turned in on themselves, the way the inner curves seemed to both cut through and go over and under the outer lines at the same time. He knew it from somewhere inside of him, but he also recalled seeing it at the museum. In one of the smaller back rooms. In the curiosities section.

"Wasn't that," he began, as it came back to him, "wasn't that same pattern on two little bottles?"

"Yes!" exclaimed Anna. "You're right. There were two vials, weren't there? Two little copper vials—one was really dark, almost brown, and the other was a really light orangey-red."

"And they both had that pattern on them, sort of raised up, bright," added Bengt.

"Don't they sound just like the type of thing you could keep tears in?" chipped in Nils.

"Oh, Nils, yes!" said Anna. "They could hold the tears of a pure-hearted warrior, shed in sorrow on this side of the veil..."

Bengt turned to William. "Does that pattern mean anything?" he asked.

William nodded. "It's a soul seal. It's the symbol of the True Dreamers." He looked at Bengt knowingly.

Bengt stared back at William but said nothing. He wished so much he could grab those scattered memories that were just under the surface;

wished he knew why this William Wynn seemed so familiar; wished he knew why the sword felt good in his hand, made him feel more... complete, somehow. He knew that *Jack Broadsword* was only a name he had made up, but he didn't think he could have made up someone like William Wynn.

"Hey!" shouted an angry voice, and Bengt turned to see Frasier McCurdey standing at the door of The Tartan Teapot, which they were passing. Mr Broadchip had been joined by the late-night rush of Lucas Whetstone, old Winnie Hawkins, Amjad Ali and a confused-looking family of four, who'd got off at the the wrong bus stop and now had to wait an hour and a half for the next bus. Everyone looked up at the noise. "What's some wee bairn doing with a big old sword like that?"

"I-I..." stuttered Bengt, as he kept on walking.

"The whole wide world's gone sword crazy tonight," went on Mr McCurdey. "Tell your other sword-waving friend he's not welcome back here! Found scratches on my floor where he'd been dragging that humongous great thing. Taking liberties. Taking liberties with my floor, it is!" He started to raise his fist at Bengt as the confused boy hurried to catch up with the others.

"Dad," said Isla McCurdey, pulling her father back from the door, "calm down, for heaven's sake. You're upsetting poor Mr Broadchip, and he's only just calmed down from all the noise earlier. He's still stuck on seventeen down."

"Is it national sword day or something? National sword day, and nobody told me? Is seventeen-down a five-letter word for sharp, dangerous weapon that scratches hardworking café owners' floors? Blooming should be, today!"

The confused-looking family of four started to look quite uncomfortable, but the Uppington Down regulars, Mr Broadchip aside, were quite used to Frasier McCurdey's outbursts by now. The incident with the French tourists, Mr McCurdey's trousers and the misunderstanding over the trifle had become a thing of local legend.

"Dad!" insisted Isla, pulling her father inside and closing the door. Her eyes followed William Wynn through the big glass window and down the street towards the museum.

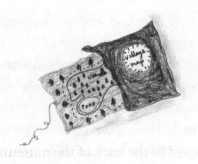

CHAPTER 38

It was after seven thirty now and the museum was supposed to be shut. But lights could be seen on inside, and the large front doors were standing slightly ajar. William made his way towards them. He turned to his companions.

"Quiet," he whispered. "Goblin, leave your hound here."

Then he slipped through the heavy front doors. Gribblebob bent to tie Dimple up, as the three children followed William into the museum.

The entrance itself was dark, but they could just make out the sign—*Welcome to the Past! Come and discover the history of Uppington Down and its surrounds*—and there was a relief map of the village and the surrounding countryside and hills.

The light was bleeding out from one of the side rooms, farther back.

"That's where they keep the curiosities," whispered Anna.

"Yes," breathed Bengt, "that's where those copper bottles were."

They moved to the back of the museum, towards the light, and they could hear a scratching and a scattering behind the door. William reached out and placed his slender fingers around the handle, then gently opened it. The light spilled out from the room, and they saw a very strange sight in front of them.

There was a straight-backed man dressed rather like Anna imagined an old-fashioned bank manager would dress: fine, dark-blue three-piece suit, shoes shinier than a wedding-day limousine, crisp white collar and cuffs edging out sharply from the blue of the suit, dizzying bright-gold cufflinks, and a powder-blue silk explosion of a tie with a single silver tie pin. A short-back-and-sides haircut from a 1930s film on the TV, black hair parted and oiled, office-pale skin that looked like it had never seen the sun and eyes as blue and as exploded as his tie. The man was bent slightly over a museum exhibit, at such an angle that they couldn't quite see what he was doing. Behind him, there seemed to be three or four shifting, dancing shapes, blurring in and out of focus.

"Rip-riders," Anna said, terrified.

The bank-manager man looked up and smiled.

"Oh, how perfectly marvellous," he said, putting down whatever it was he had in his hand and turning round to face them properly. The sharp-edged man then clapped his hands once in delight and repeated: "Marvellous! If it isn't William Wynn, out on a delightful little outing, I'd venture. And what is it that he's brought with him on the trip? Why, if it isn't one of the most unpleasant goblins I've ever had the misfortune to encounter, two rather bland children and"—he took sight of Bengt for the first time—"and one of you. Oh, what fun we'll have. Thank you, William, you have so made my day."

"Hobley," said William carefully. "I had you down as a bad sort, but doing the Rider's work? That's a dark journey, even for you."

"William," he said, stressing the final syllable and consonant. "I do my queen's bidding. And, my, if you only knew what I've been promised. If you had only seen the things Maya has shown me. If you had only tasted just one sweet drop of what I have drunk of... then you'd understand."

The rip-riders hissed and shifted behind him.

"You can't be a-trusting that one," said Gribblebob. "She'll turn you up and down and round five times before breakfast and still not boil your egg."

Hobley Brown giggled. "Oh, my lovely little man. You are such a tonic. Truly unpleasant in all the best ways. You do make a weary heart smile."

"He's right," said William. "You can't trust her. And if you open the book, if you unbind the spell, do you really want all that on your conscience? All the nightmares back. All the terror. All the hurt. Is it worth doing what she wants?"

"Sweet William Wynn, we all do the bidding of others, do we not? We all have our masters and our mistresses and our paymasters and our homework-givers. Is that not true, bland children?" Hobley said, addressing the children directly now. "Don't you have Wednesday night homework to do? Oh, I think by the time I've finished playing with you, you'll all be wishing you had stayed home eating eggy soldiers and doing your nine times table."

Anna could see that Hobley had in front of him an ancient-looking book, which she guessed must be *The Book of All Tomorrow's Dreams*, and she could also see the two small bottles she and Bengt had remembered, though they were more like very small vases, with long stems but bulbous bottoms.

"It's them!" she shouted, pointing.

"Why, yes, you dull little girl, that's exactly right. And, do you know, that's most probably the last boring thing you'll ever get to say of your own accord. Take them."

The last two words appeared to be spoken to the writhing forms around him, and as the last breath left his lips, the rip-riders flew towards William, Gribblebob and the children.

CHAPTER 39

As the screeching spirits came furiously towards them, Nils started to shake with the most unbridled terror he had ever felt, and he took a step back involuntarily. But at the same time as he stepped back, he felt his hand, the one that had Gribblebob's book trapped in it, start to rise. He couldn't stop it—in the same way as he couldn't stop the shaking and he couldn't stop himself stepping back in fear, he now couldn't stop his hand rising. As it rose, he also felt himself start to walk—no, run—forwards, in front of William and the others. Faster than he would have believed possible.

"Oh, look," laughed Hobley Brown, "the tedious boy is so eager for a bit of magic in his life that he is just rushing to be ripped into. What a monotone life they live this side of the veil."

The rip-riders rushed forwards to Nils and the others, but somehow he felt sure of what he had to do. He knew it, in the same way he knew his parents loved him and that his sister would lay down her life for him. He held up his other hand, so both hands were raised out in front of him, and then he spread his fingers. The scrolling text spooled across his left hand and seemed to leap across the empty air to his right hand, creating some sort of shield of words between the two. The spooling letters and words and names moved quicker and quicker, jumping from one hand to the other then back again, like a tumble dryer of words held in the space in front of him.

Faster and faster, a tsunami of text was rushing in the air between his hands, and Nils could feel its power. He could feel the magic the Great Goblin had used to bind the names in the book, the magic needed to act as a warning about the dark shadowfolk and unpleasant goblins contained within its pages. The magic of light that bound the darkness.

As the rip-riders approached, the swirling rush of words acted like a kind of magical vacuum cleaner, starting to suck the wraiths towards it. Nils began to stumble as he saw the ragged faces and haunted eyes and wailing mouths of the rip-riders come near him. He could hear the terror of the nightmares they lived in, could hear it echo in the space behind his ears. For just a moment, he started to doubt himself. He felt the dead-of-night loneliness of a real nightmare start to whisper to him. He felt the stirrings of a nightmare where his parents didn't love him and his sister laughed at him as he lay floating away on a barge full of unwanted children, heading down a dirty-water canal towards a factory yard full of chimneys, towards coal mines and empty beds and useless rhymes. His hands started to drop, the whirl of words in front of him started to diminish, started to falter, and the rip-riders began to pull away from the suction force of it, shrieking in sad victory.

Anna didn't know what was happening, but she saw her brother—her brave little brother, pure of thought and good of heart—standing there facing the rip-riders, and she saw his arm drop, and she saw him stumble and falter, and she did what she always did when she saw her little brother stumble or fall or falter. She rushed to him, to help him up. She took the hand that had dropped, feeling it shaking slightly in hers, and gripped it tight. She felt the skin that was her skin, and the blood that was her blood, and the love that was her love, and she gripped it even tighter, and she felt how strong they were together.

Nils gripped back. He felt his sister's love—he felt her support and all the times she had been there for him—and the beginnings of the nightmare drifted away; the barge and the canal and the laughter stopped. Once again he felt his family's love, and he raised his hand, still gripping tightly to his sister's, and the maelstrom of letters and words and names grew quicker again, and blew and sucked, and the rip-riders shrieked and screamed as they were pulled into the reverse hurricane that Nils and Anna produced between them.

All of a sudden the rip-riders were gone, and the swirl of words stopped—with a loud implosion, a huge *pop*—and Nils shouted, "OWWW!" and let go of Anna's hand and fell to the floor. There was a sound like paper rustling, then a rainbow beam of text came flooding out of Nils's hand and arced through the air towards Gribblebob's waistcoat pocket, where his empty *Book of Unpleasant Goblins* lay resting. There was a crackle of fire and paper as the beam hit, and then the goblin reached in and took out the book.

"Got me book back," he said, smiling, "and with a few extra names in, I'll wager a badger to a pea."

"Nils!" shouted Anna, lifting up his head. "Nils, are you okay?"

"Oh, pip-a-doodle," said Hobley Brown. "That's most disquieting."

CHAPTER 40

William looked over and could see that Nils was okay, with Anna's arm around him.

"I wouldn't call that dull," he said, with the hint of a smile.

Hobley Brown waved a hand dismissively.

"Merely a sideshow," he said, as he picked up one of the two small bottles. "Do you know what these are, William Wynn? Do you know what these little lovelies contain?"

"Sure as a shoreline you'll be telling us right enough," said Gribblebob.

"Oh, I will, you most unpleasant little goblin, I will. These pretty little trinkets hold a greater treasure than the blind fools who run this place know."

"What a blabbering baloney you are, a bore-in-one."

Hobley Brown glared at the goblin.

"A very long time ago there was some... unpleasantness... this side of the veil, involving—"

Gribblebob made a show of yawning loudly.

"Well, never mind. Suffice to say that two warriors from our side broke the veil and put right what needed to be put right. But what they had to do brought them to tears, so as a remembrance of what they had wrought, and as a warning to others who came after, they collected their tears in these vials. They say the reflection of the horrors they saw are still visible in the tears. A spell was placed on them, to help protect this side of the veil, and they were left here. How perfectly lucky for me! All I need to do now is use their tears to wash this book. And then? Oh, and then..."

Before anyone could say anything, Hobley Brown broke off the stem of the darker bottle and tipped the tears it contained over *The Book of All Tomorrow's Dreams*, which steamed and fizzed and stirred as the liquid touched it.

"Stop!" shouted William.

"Oh, I doubt that I'm going to stop. I doubt that very much indeed," said Hobley, smiling, and reached for the second vial.

CHAPTER 41

There was a flutter and flash of wings and claws and teeth, and a dark shape flew through the museum towards Hobley Brown.

Rather than flinch from the oncoming creature, as most others would have done, Hobley merely smiled.

"Oh, how darling," he commented.

Just as the furious, dark thing was nearly on him, he muttered something bitter and stale under his breath, and up out of what had been nothing but shadows and dust, up out of the echoed places that we only see out of the corner of our eye, rose something vile and vicious and violent, like a night-water shimmer, directly in front of him.

As the glowing figure seemed to harden at its edges, William's otherself of wings and teeth and claws and fury flew right into it. He completely disappeared for a moment, throwing out splinters of crackled light from the shimmer. There was a keening screech, wild and ancient, hungry and eager, and then the flying beast was spat out by the strange figure just as quickly as it had flown into it. The otherself fell to the floor and rolled over, then rolled over once more and it was William again, in his red frock coat and scuffed boots and long hair, looking shaken and drained.

"My queen protects me, you see," laughed Hobley, picking up the second vial.

William, shivering, looked up and saw, there in the air by Hobley Brown, something he had never thought it was possible to see. It was Mara, the Rider. She looked like a thousand rip-riders in one. More solid than them, but still wraith-like, immaterial. Like a deep, dark pool of water at night. Half unseen and menacing. She glistened and glittered, an evil beauty. Her hair was long trails of that dusky sunlight that bleeds into shadow, her fingernails sharp thorns of black roses, her lips the siren call of drowning sailors. She opened her mouth to speak, and each word was made up of the screams of a thousand lost nights... ten thousand, more. William flinched from the sound. He couldn't make out the words, but he knew what Mara was saying: *I win. I return.*

"Blimey," said Gribblebob.

To everyone's surprise, most especially his, Bengt Arbuthnot strode forward, the broadsword in his hand.

"Oh, how precious," sneered Hobley at Bengt. "He thinks he's a hero. I thought I could smell it on him. What a pretty sight he'll be once my queen shreds him." He looked away dismissively, back down at the second vial in his hand.

Bengt thought about all his made-up names. About being brave. About defeating nasty bullies like Mandy Musgrave. He thought about the broadsword in his hand and how natural it felt. He could sense... possibilities within himself. He thought about what a hero like Jack Broadsword would say and do if his good friend William Wynn was lying beaten on the ground, if Mara the Rider was about to unleash a plague of nightmares on the land and if a smartly dressed smarm-merchant like Hobley Brown was about to open a copper vial containing the tears of a pure-hearted warrior.

"No," he said, "I won't let this happen."

Hobley Brown threw back his head and laughed. "You? You won't let this happen? I can smell what you are inside, but you're still only a boy. A bland little boy with a big man's sword. And I am Hobley Brown, servant to my queen—Mara the Rider, queen of nightmare, ruler of terror."

At this, Mara's black light shimmered even darker, and she too seemed to be laughing.

"Who are you next to her?"

Bengt was actually rather tired of being laughed at. He was tired of Mandy and her gang and all those others, even the teachers sometimes, laughing at him, and—to be quite frank—he wasn't going to take it any more.

He searched inside himself. And he found Jack Broadsword. He found Jack, and he found Oscar Oakheart and William Summerksy, and perhaps most importantly, right there, right then, he found Bengt Arbuthnot.

Bengt walked calmly forwards towards Mara and Hobley, who was holding the second vial tightly in his hand.

"Who am I?" He ignored Mara and looked directly at the man holding the vial, who despite himself could not stop looking into Bengt's eyes and seeing something that troubled him there. "Who am I?" he repeated. "I am Bengt Arbuthnot"—and he said his name proudly, probably for the first time ever in his life—"and I am..." He paused, and for a moment he wanted to say 'I am Jack Broadsword'. And, just as he thought that, all those scattered memories, those echoes inside him, the feeling of something coming alive—somehow everything ignited in him and the words simply flowed out: "I am a pure-hearted warrior of the True Dreamers, and you are going to remember today as the day that I vanquished you and your petty little queen."

"Wh-what?" stammered Hobley. There was something about Bengt's voice, something about the words he said and the way he said them, something about the way he was standing and the way he held the sword, that seemed to affect Hobley. It froze him and stopped him from opening the vial.

Bengt took a step towards Mara, who shrieked and shook her blackness at him, her long fingernails clawing at the boy—to take his eyes, to rip into his cheek—but he simply raised the sword in front of his face and her nails clinked against the metal. She pulled her hand back in pain.

"It-it's not possible." Hobley Brown started to shake a little.

Bengt walked on, and again, from deep inside him came a voice that was his, but which carried the echo of another.

"Mara, you may be queen of nightmare, but you only have power when you feast on the dreams of others. And dreams, real dreams, pure dreams—dreams of a better world and a kinder world—aren't just dreams to be had at night in bed. Those are dreams to have in the light too, and those dreams will always, always be more powerful than nightmares. And do you know why?"

Now Bengt had walked past Mara, ignoring her hissing and her bile, and was striding towards Hobley, who looked at him in shocked horror.

"I'll tell you why, Hobley Brown. It's because nightmares exist in an absence of hope, but dreams—pure dreams, true dreams—they breathe in the air of hope, they flourish in the world of possibilities and opportunities and a longing for a brighter and a better tomorrow."

Bengt had reached Hobley. He leant forward and took the copper bottle, and Hobley's shaking hand put up no resistance.

"True dreams burn away nightmares, in the pure, beautiful knowledge"—and here Bengt laid down his sword, broke the top of the vial and held it to his lips—"that hope and belief and love will always vanquish fear and hate and darkness. And so today"—and now Bengt drank down the tears held in the bottle, so that they could never ever bathe the book—"today I vanquish you."

And with that, Mara was gone.

CHAPTER 42

When Mara left, the whole atmosphere in the museum changed—like when the lights go up at the end of a film and you see, oh yes, you were just in a cinema the whole time—and so now, oh yes, they were just in the Uppington Down Museum of Antiquities and Curiosities the whole time. On a Wednesday. Long after closing time.

When Hobley saw that Mara was gone, he went to grab *The Book of All Tomorrow's Dreams*, but Bengt placed his hand firmly on the cover, and Hobley stepped back. He looked into Bengt's eyes and saw something there, maybe the hard truth of who he was reflected back at him, or maybe even a glimmer of the horrors in the tears from the vial, and he shivered some more, and whimpered, and turned, and went running out of the museum.

Gribblebob moved to stop him, but William Wynn shouted faintly: "Let him go."

Anna and Nils stood up and went over to William, who managed to rouse himself to his feet too. They looked over at Bengt, who was standing with *The Book of All Tomorrow's Dreams* in his hands.

"Wow," said Nils, "that was awesome."

"Incredible," said Anna, thinking of the timid boy she had seen bullied by Mandy Musgrave.

"I-I don't really know what happened," said Bengt sheepishly. "I just thought about what Jack Broadsword might do or say, and all that poured out."

William grinned. "That is *exactly* what my friend Jack Broadsword would have said and done." He held out his hand and Bengt gave him the book. "And now we need to get this book to a proper book-keeper."

CHAPTER 43

As they made their way down the high street, back to the school library, they passed The Tartan Teapot again. Had it really only been a little over an hour ago that they'd passed it the other way? So much had happened. The tea shop was empty of customers now. Mr Broadchip was just leaving, his newspaper tucked under his arm, the crossword happily completed for another day. Frasier McCurdey was bidding him goodbye when he noticed the strange band of companions walking by.

"Heather in the highlands!" he exclaimed. "Here they come again. Up and down. Back and forth. All outside my café with their swords and their sabres and their sassiness. Taunting me, they are. Taunting me."

Hearing his raised voice, Isla came to the door. The confused family of four were waiting at the bus stop across the street. They shrunk back together at the sound of the loud Scottish voice, to avoid attracting his attention. They had only gone into the café for something to drink, but the crazed owner had somehow got them to order four leek and potato soups, two bread and butter puddings, a raspberry tart and a slice of clootie dumpling. Enough was enough.

"Not again, Dad," said Isla. "Didn't we just speak about this? Find your happy place. Zonal breathing, remember?"

"Don't you start with all that happy-clappy nonsense again. I know when I'm being provoked." He narrowed his eyes and stared intently at the group as they walked by. The children shrunk into themselves, avoiding his gaze, William nodded his head at Isla and unleashed that smile, Dimple sniffed around for ginger-snap crumbs, only the very top of his head missing now, and Gribblebob glowered at Mr McCurdey, who flicked his eyes at Dimple.

"You should get that dog looked at," he said.

"Oh, mind your own bedstead," Gribblebob snapped. "It's your weak-as-whimsy badcurrant juice that needs cooking at."

"Right. You cheeky..." began the café owner, starting out the door, but his daughter held on to his arm, pulling him back from the doorway.

"Dad," said Isla. "Dad, what are we going to do with you?" And she watched the back of William Wynn's head once more, as he walked down the road, wondering if she was ever going to see him again. There was something about him...

"Let's not walk this way any more today," said Nils, his hand in Anna's. "I don't think poor Mr McCurdey could take it."

Gribblebob snorted.

"That one couldn't bake a bunny on a biscuit," he said, and Anna and Nils looked at each other and shrugged again.

"William," said Bengt. "Back in the museum, when I went up against Mara, all the things I said... somehow I just knew what to say. It was like they were in me, just waiting to be released. I really felt like a pure-hearted warrior. I really felt like... like I was Jack Broadsword, or he was me, or something."

"He's one of *them*, ain't he?" said Gribblebob to William.

"One of what?" asked Bengt, worried.

William sighed.

"There are True Dreamers on both sides of the veil. When the veil first appeared, families were split asunder, broken up. So it meant that, even on your side of the veil, the old-blood families existed and carried on. As the years went by, in a world without magic and spells and—"

"Dragon poo," interjected the goblin, but William ignored him and continued.

"In such a world, it was easy to lose touch with who you really were. But True Dreamers remained close to the veil, even though they didn't know it."

"And there are some fuzzy spots," Gribblebob added, "where the veil is weak and wobbly."

"And so, some people," William took over again, "True Dreamers like you, when they are near such places, whisperings and flutterings get through. You hear things, pick things up from the other side, without even realizing it."

"So I've been picking things up from your world. All my made-up names? My stories?"

William nodded. "And also I think that, due to some odd quirk in the veil-magic, you and Jack are connected, entwined, part of each other."

"Bit of a mist tree," said Gribblebob, scratching the back of his head. "Well, actually, more like two trees sharing the same roots." He paused and looked up at Bengt. "You True Dreamers ain't magic, but you feel it. You are sucky-table to it."

"Uh, susceptible?" Bengt raised a questioning eyebrow.

"Pre-slicely. And when magic is on the move, when things in the dreamworld are wild and woolly, then True Dreamers are needed."

William gave Bengt a warm look. "Yes, when *The Book of All Tomorrow's Dreams* was taken and there was trouble in the air, it stirred things up. And there must have been some benefit to be had by you and Jack coming together, for a little while at least. It wasn't only Jack's warrior spirit that defeated Mara. It was your pure heart. Jack fought in the Sapphire Wars: he's done things a warrior needs to do, seen things that a soldier sees. Those dark things could have been a weakness when facing Mara. She could have turned them back on Jack. It was a weakness you didn't have. When you came together, it opened up both you and Jack. You feel him more now, and I daresay he feels you more."

Bengt was quiet for a few seconds, taking everything in, before saying: "So when the Grey Lady said Jack had been here, on this side of the veil, for a very long time..."

"She meant that a part of Jack has always been in you, and a part of you in him," William said, nodding, "so there was no real sign of him having crossed over. He was always here, in you."

"I'd love to meet him one day," said Bengt.

"You know, I'm not sure if that would work," said William, scratching his cheek. "I'm not sure if you two could actually be together in the same place, at the same time. The link you have seems to be so strong, so powerful, I wonder if it might not cause problems if you were ever to meet."

"The veil is a rumplestillyskin thing at times," said Gribblebob wisely. "Ain't not nobody can really make shed nor sail out of it."

"But do you think Jack's safe? Do you think he's okay back on your side of the veil?" asked Bengt.

"I'm sure of it." William smiled kindly. "But look, we're here."

And indeed, they were now standing outside the school library again.

CHAPTER 44

As Gribblebob tied up Dimple outside the library, he gave him the very last lick of ginger-snap crumbs he had in his pocket, and the dog's whole head shimmered into view.

"There's my beautiful boy," Gribblebob said, tickling Dimple's ears.

"He just looks like a normal dog," said Nils, sounding slightly disappointed.

"What did you expect? Tusks and horns? He's a shadowdog, not a ruddy warthound, you know."

"Do warthounds have tusks and horns, then?" asked Anna, intrigued.

"Come on, let's go inside and see how Omeria is faring," said William, before Gribblebob could answer.

Inside the library, Ms Toureau seemed much better. She was walking around, albeit a little stiffly, picking up books here and there, but you could barely see the marks on her face now. When they entered, she let out a huge sigh and closed her eyes for a moment.

"I am so relieved to see all of you, so relieved."

"Ms Toureau," said Anna, moving towards the librarian. "Are you okay?"

"Yes, sweet." She nodded. "Your brother chose that book of protection wisely. In a few days, I'll be perfectly fine again, which is more than I can say of my poor library." She looked sadly around the devastated room.

"How on earth are you going to explain all this to Mr Cobbister?" asked Bengt.

"Hmm. I haven't had time to think about it. Electrical power surge? Air conditioning explosion causing an indoor tornado? Overdue book maybe?" She tilted her head quizzically to one side and grinned broadly at the children. "I'll think of something."

"Bookworms," blurted Gribblebob. "Tell him it was bookworms that done it. Big snakey ones."

"Well," she said, raising one eyebrow at the goblin, "perhaps."

"But most of the books look okay, anyway," said Nils. "That's good news."

"Books endure, sweet," said the librarian, nodding in agreement. "Books endure."

"Talking of books that endure..." said William, taking a step forward and holding out *The Book of All Tomorrow's Dreams*. "I think we need a bookkeeper to take care of this."

Omeria Toureau took the heavy tome from William with both hands and held it tight to her chest.

"Thank you, Mr Wynn." After holding it close to her for some seconds, she ran one hand gently down the spine of the book, and then over the thick cover, where the spilled tears from the first vial had left a ragged scar. "Yes, this one has had a narrow escape today, to be sure."

"Will you see that it gets back to where it belongs?" asked William.

"Of course," replied Omeria. "But aren't you crossing back across the veil yourself?"

"I am, but I have something much more important to return."

William turned to Bengt and held out his hand, nodding towards the broadsword that the boy still carried at his side. "May I?"

Bengt handed over the sword to William, feeling a little bit sad to be letting go of it.

"Thank you, young sir. I need to get this back safe to our... mutual friend," he explained, and he winked at Bengt.

"Are you absolutely certain you don't wish to return the book yourself, Mr Wynn?" questioned Ms Toureau. "I'm sure that the"—she looked over at the children and chose her words carefully—"powers-that-be... would be extremely grateful to have the book returned safely."

William sighed. "True, very true." He turned the broadsword over in his hands, looking down at it, feeling the weight of it, feeling Jack in it. "But some things are worth more than gratitude and reward." He looked up at Omeria. "No, thank you, fair lady. You return the book. I want to make haste and place this back in the hand it belongs."

"Careful of the Court of Naughtiness," said Nils. "You don't want to be carved into a statue."

"A statue?" said William in surprise, and looked over at Gribblebob. "Have you been telling your tall tales again, Bobblehead?"

Nils and Anna laughed, and Bengt wondered what they were going on about.

"What about Hobley Brown?" he asked.

"Yeah, what about that flimming grimblesnort?" grumbled Gribblebob.

"He'll pay his dues," William said sternly.

"And Mara?" asked Anna.

"She's around, she's out there. Mara's angry and resentful. But she lost the chance to get her full power back, so... so... so that's all there is to say about that. And now, I must be on my way."

"But aren't we going to break the veil?" said Nils. "I want to see what it's like."

"Yes!" exclaimed Anna. "We must go now, after hearing all about it. You promised." She looked over at Gribblebob.

"Young fella-me-lad's hand is all mended. Me book is back in its right and proper. No treason for you to go now."

"But..." began Anna.

"What about you, Ms Toureau?" asked Nils. "Can't we go with you when you take the book back?"

The librarian shook her head. "I'm afraid I don't think that's an awfully good idea."

"Tell you what," sighed Gribblebob. "I got me some extra chapters in me book now, so I'll need to break the veil with it one day soon and take it with me to get the Great Goblin to sort it out.

If you don't make too much of a fuzz out of it, maybe I might see fit to bring you with me on a little sneaky-snakey visit."

"Gribblebob..." warned William.

"Mr Gribble..." echoed Ms Toureau.

"Well, we'll see-saw."

Anna and Nils looked at each other. Without having to say anything, they both understood that keeping quiet now was probably their best bet of one day taking a trip with the goblin.

Instead, Anna only said, "Nils, it must be well past nine o'clock now—we should get home before Mum and Dad get back or we'll have a lot of explaining to do, and I don't think I'd know where to start."

And so, with that, they said their goodbyes and parted, with Mr Cobbister the caretaker blissfully unaware of the unholy mess that lay waiting for him in the library the following day.

CHAPTER 45

Jack Broadsword had slept for what seemed a very long and very deep time. He woke with a start and a gasp. He reached for his sword, and it wasn't there. What trickery was this? He jumped up from under the tree and felt dizzy. He reached out a hand to steady himself. He had broken the veil, hadn't he? That hadn't been a dream. With that trickster ex-friend of his, William Wynn. And they had been in a school library, and it had felt wrong and scary and...

"Hello, Jack."

He looked up and William Wynn was standing there, by the clearing. He gave that full-beam smile of his.

"You're looking a little worse for wear, Jack. And you seem to be missing something." He held up his hand, and in it was Jack's treasured broadsword.

"How?..."

"Do I have a story to tell you, my friend." As William walked towards Jack, holding out the sword to him hilt first, his smile changed slightly and he said, with real longing and pleading in his voice, "We are still friends, aren't we, Jack?"

Jack Broadsword reached for the sword, paused and looked into William's eyes. And he felt something within him that had been missing for a while, something from a deeper "him", something powerful that healed old wounds and opened new doors.

Jack reached out and took hold of the sword's hilt. "Friends, William?" he replied. "We're not friends."

William froze, still holding the shaft of the sword.

Then Jack gently pulled the sword to him, and as William released his grip, Jack carried on speaking: "We're family."

William smiled then, and it wasn't his normal, full-force, everyday smile; it was a smile that bubbled out from deep in his heart and lit his face with sunshine and warmth. William blinked away a tear and sat down next to Jack on the soft, warm grass.

"Well, I knew you couldn't go on resisting my charming nature for too long, Jack," he said, winking, and Jack Broadsword shook his head and laughed.

CHAPTER 46

The next day, at lunchtime, Bengt was walking with Anna in the school cafeteria, each carrying a tray. He liked her, she seemed kind and warm, and they certainly had a lot to talk about. On their way to lunch they'd had to go by Mr Cobbister the caretaker's room, and they'd looked at each other knowingly as they saw the sign he had pinned to his door:

IN LIBRARY FOR FORESEEABLE FUTURE.

Oh dear.

As they walked to find a place at a table, they had to go past Mandy and her giggling gang.

"Well, look who it isn't," she sneered. "Benny Butt'n'hole." Her entourage cheered and laughed.

"And it looks like he's gone and got himself a girlfriend—little Pippi Longstocking there." Again, the laughter broke out. "What is it then, has she got a thing for stupid-name losers or does she just feel sorry for you?"

"Oh, do be quiet, Mandy," snapped Anna.

"Ooooh," pantomimed Mandy. "Little Benny's got a bodyguard girlfriend. Sweet!"

Bengt stopped walking, and Anna, next to him, could feel his body tense.

"He doesn't need a bodyguard," said Anna loudly and with real passion. Mandy and her gang sniggered, and Mandy was about to say something else, when Bengt turned sharply and took a few steps towards where she was sitting. Mandy Musgrave seemed taken aback that Bengt was actually going to say something to her.

"What? Got something to say for yourself, have you, Benny-boy?"

Bengt stood directly in front of Mandy's table and said nothing; he just looked at her. Anna felt that he was looking at Mandy in rather the same way he'd been looking at Hobley Brown the day before, and she actually found herself being just a little concerned for Mandy. But not too much.

"What? What is it, weirdo?" the bully said. "Are you going to ask me out too?" Her gang laughed, but to be honest she was feeling a bit creeped out by the way he was looking at her.

"Mandy Musgrave," he finally said, and sighed. "Mandy, Mandy Musgrave." He shook his head sadly from side to side. There were a few scattered chuckles, but most of Mandy's table were really surprised and wondering what was going on.

"Spit it out, then," she said. "Or I'll spit it out for you."

Which actually didn't mean anything, if you thought about it.

"Do you know, Mandy, why you're such a bully? Do you understand why you need to be nasty and rude to people who are quieter and smaller than you? Why you need to be horrible to people who don't stand up to you?"

"Move along, A-butt-thong, you're boring me," she said, but she looked a little worried.

"It's because somewhere you're empty inside. It's because somehow you're much more scared and lonely than you can ever let on. It's because somehow you don't feel loved, or looked at, or liked, or cared for, or somehow you don't even feel anything. And it's only by hitting out, by saying horrible things to people, that you get to feel anything, that you actually feel you matter."

Mandy stood up from the table and went for Bengt. "You are in such trouble now, you ugly little runt!"

Bengt stood his ground. "You're weak, Mandy. And every time you bully someone, you show it. It's like a beacon flashing over your head. *Weak. Weak. Weak.*"

Mandy didn't say anything, instead she lunged at Bengt with her fists and her kicking legs.

Bengt calmly took a step back, flipping his tray over quickly, so it was like a shield. Of course everything on the tray went flying off towards the advancing Mandy, who was quickly covered in orange juice, gravy, bits of chicken and rice and chocolate tapioca pudding, just as her fist weakly hit the tray.

She shrieked at him in anger and frustration, and scooped a piece of chocolatey chicken away from her forehead as it dangled from her fringe and the gravy oozed down her cheeks.

"Oops," said Bengt softly. "Butterfingers, me." And then he dropped the tray to the ground with a clatter, which sounded amazingly loud in the now pin-drop quiet cafeteria.

Everyone was looking at Bengt and Mandy.

"Sorry about that," said Bengt, before gently nudging Anna's arm. "Come on, maybe I can share some of your lunch."

Mandy and her gang watched them depart in shocked amazement, and Mandy's enablers looked at her slightly differently.

"That was amazing," Anna whispered to him.

"Mandy Musgrave may be a bully," Bengt whispered back, "but she's no Mara."

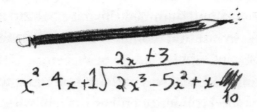

$$x^2 - 4x + 1 \overline{\smash{\big)}\, 2x^3 - 5x^2 + x} \quad \dfrac{2x+3}{10}$$

CHAPTER 47

That night, Anna was doing her homework at the kitchen table when she saw Nils slip on his coat by the back door.

"Where are you going?" she asked, her pencil resting on her lips as she still half thought about the maths problem.

"I'm, uh, I'm going to go and visit Gribblebob. He said I could. I said I'd help him walk Dimple. And I want to make sure that he hasn't forgotten about his promise to take us across the veil one day."

"But haven't you got homework to do too?"

"Oh, I can do it later, it's simple. Only got to write a poem about badgers or baboons or something."

"Nils, you should do your homework first."

"Oh, don't be such a flimming grimblesnort, sis," he said, and slammed the door behind him.

It was in just that moment Anna had the feeling that Robert Gribble Esquire of Webstone Cottage, Blacksmith's Lane, was perhaps not going to be a terribly good influence on her little brother.

And she went back to her long division.

Acknowledgements

I'd just like to say how grateful I am to Adam Freudenheim and his excellent team at Pushkin Press for helping ease a first-time author through the book publishing process.

Firstly, of course, I have to say a massive "thank you" to Sarah Odedina for showing an interest in my story and for advice and encouragement in turning it into a book. She's always been so positive and helpful along the way and I couldn't have asked for a better or nicer editor.

Tilda Johnson was a fantastic copy editor and gave me lots of great suggestions for little tweaks here and there, and the book is much better because of her.

I am so happy with the fabulous illustrations from Jen Khatun, the cover and the chapter headings really help bring the book to life and Anna Morrison's design work has really turned the story into a book. The rest of the behind-the-scenes people have also been so friendly and helpful and really supportive, so a big thank you to India Darsley, Managing Editor, Mollie Stewart, Publicity and Marketing Officer and Rory Williamson, Editorial Assistant.

I wrote *Gribblebob's Book of Unpleasant Goblins* one or two chapters at a time, in order, and read them as bedtime stories to my children, Sam and Tilly, who gave me huge amounts of great ideas for what might happen next and told me when things were getting boring. Thank you! I love you.

My wife, Elvira, is also an author and she helped me tremendously with the book too, giving me lots of encouragement and suggestions and making it easy for me to write. You ARE the best and without you there'd be nothing. XXX

Finally, just a heartfelt thanks to Bengta Andersson and Mathias Sautermeister for being such good friends and being so helpful in so many ways. Tack!

PUSHKIN CHILDREN'S BOOKS

We created Pushkin Children's Books to share tales from different languages and cultures with younger readers, and to open the door to the wide, colourful worlds these stories offer.

From picture books and adventure stories to fairy tales and classics, and from fifty-year-old bestsellers to current huge successes abroad, the books on the Pushkin Children's list reflect the very best stories from around the world, for our most discerning readers of all: children.

THE BEGINNING WOODS
MALCOLM MCNEILL

'I loved every word and was envious of quite a few... A
modern classic. Rich, funny and terrifying'
Eoin Colfer

THE TUNNELS BELOW
NADINE WILD-PALMER

'A hugely imaginative debut with a brilliantly resourceful heroine.'
Fiona Noble, *The Bookseller*

THE LETTER FOR THE KING
TONKE DRAGT

'*The Letter for the King* will get pulses racing... Pushkin
Press deserves every praise for publishing this beautifully
translated, well-presented and captivating book'
The Times

THE SECRETS OF THE WILD WOOD
TONKE DRAGT

'Offers intrigue, action and escapism'
Sunday Times

THE SONG OF SEVEN
TONKE DRAGT

'A cracking adventure...
so nail-biting you'll need to wear protective gloves'
The Times

THE MURDERER'S APE
JAKOB WEGELIUS

'A thrilling adventure. Prepare to meet the remarkable
Sally Jones; you won't soon forget her'
Publishers Weekly

THE PARENT TRAP · THE FLYING CLASSROOM · DOT AND ANTON

ERICH KÄSTNER

Illustrated by Walter Trier

'The bold line drawings by Walter Trier are the work of
genius... As for the stories, if you're a fan of *Emil and the
Detectives*, then you'll find these just as spirited'

Spectator

FROM THE MIXED-UP FILES OF MRS. BASIL E. FRANKWEILER

E. L. KONIGSBURG

'Delightful... I love this book... a beautifully written
adventure, with endearing characters and full of dry
wit, imagination and inspirational confidence'

Daily Mail

THE RECKLESS SERIES

CORNELIA FUNKE

1 · *The Petrified Flesh*

2 · *Living Shadows*

3 · *The Golden Yarn*

'A wonderful storyteller'

Sunday Times

THE WILDWITCH SERIES

LENE KAABERBØL

1 · *Wildfire*

2 · *Oblivion*

3 · *Life Stealer*

4 · *Bloodling*

'Classic fantasy adventure... Young readers will be delighted to
hear that there are more adventures to come for Clara'

Lovereading

MEET AT THE ARK AT EIGHT!

ULRICH HUB

Illustrated by Jörg Mühle

'Of all the books about a penguin in a suitcase
pretending to be God asking for a cheesecake, this
one is absolutely, definitely my favourite'
Independent

THE SNOW QUEEN

HANS CHRISTIAN ANDERSEN

Illustrated by Lucie Arnoux

'A lovely edition [of a] timeless story'
The Lady

THE WILD SWANS

HANS CHRISTIAN ANDERSEN

'A fresh new translation of these two classic fairy tales
recreates the lyrical beauty and pathos of the
Danish genius' evergreen stories'
The Bay

THE CAT WHO CAME IN OFF THE ROOF

ANNIE M.G. SCHMIDT

'Guaranteed to make anyone 7-plus to 107 who likes to
curl up with a book and a cat purr with pleasure'
The Times

LAFCADIO: THE LION WHO SHOT BACK

SHEL SILVERSTEIN

'A story which is really funny, yet also teaches us a great
deal about what we want, what we think we want and what
we are no longer certain about once we have it'
Irish Times